The Cartel 4:
Diamonds are Forever

The Cartel 4:
Diamonds are Forever

Ashley & JaQuavis

www.urbanbooks.net

Urban Books, LLC
300 Farmingdale Road, NY-Route 109
Farmingdale, NY 11735

The Cartel 4: Diamonds are Forever

ISBN 13: 978-1-62286-506-2
ISBN 10: 1-62286-506-5

First Trade Paperback Printing November 2012
Printed in the United States of America

20 19

Distributed by Kensington Publishing Corp.
Submit orders to:
Customer Service
400 Hahn Road
Westminster, MD 21157-4627
Phone: 1-800-733-3000
Fax: 1-800-659-2436

Chapter 1

"The sleeping beast had finally awoken."
                                        —Unknown

Mecca heard the sound of a gun being cocked behind him and he wasn't even startled. He didn't even turn around, for that matter. He just took a deep breath and placed his hands together in a praying form.

"Our father, which art in heaven, hallowed be thy name . . ." Mecca said as tears slid down his face. He already knew who was behind him, and it came as no surprise to him. Carter began to recite the prayer along with his brother, as he pointed the gun to the back of Mecca's head.

Mecca had always known that Carter would eventually seek revenge for Miamor's death. He had loved her way too much to not come after him. Mecca's only dilemma had been to figure out when and where Carter would take his life. Mecca was a seasoned street veteran and the one thing that he knew for sure was that "the eyes don't lie," and on that day, Carter could not hide the hatred he had inside.

Carter knew that if he let Mecca live, Mecca would possibly turn on him one day, just as he did to Monroe. He also felt obligated to avenge Miamor's death, so killing Mecca was inevitable.

Mecca also knew the game. Mecca realized that if he was in Carter's shoes, he would have done the same, so he wasn't mad at Carter for what he was about to do. Once the prayer was over, Mecca stood unflinchingly with his heart pounding through his chest. There was no malice in his heart, only regret, but he knew that his oldest brother was about to deliver his retribution.

"I love you, Carter," Mecca said as he straightened up his tie and prepared for his death.

"I love you too," Carter replied sincerely as he wrapped his finger around the trigger. "I always will, bro."

Boom!

✱✱✱

It seemed like he had heard that boom from a year ago. Slowly his senses began to be restored after a long slumber. It seemed as if he looked through Mecca's eyes just before he died. All he could see was the face of Mecca Diamond as his eyes were closed shut.

His ability to smell was the first sense that came back to him. The fresh scent from the ocean was like heaven as he took a deep inhale through his nostrils and the moist air journeyed into his lungs. Second, the sounds of the waves traveled through the air and to his ears as the waves crashed onto the shore. A light, steady beep echoed through the room from the heart monitor that sat at his bedside. The cool breeze blew through the window and caused goose bumps to form on his arm.

He took a deep breath and slowly opened his eyes. At first the sunrays were too much for his sensitive pupils, so he quickly closed them back shut. After a few seconds, he built up enough courage and tried again. He opened his eyes and his blurred vision slowly began to focus as he looked toward the open window. The beautiful ocean was in clear sight and just above it there were the blue skies; it mesmerized him.

He had been in a coma for five years and had finally come back to life. He swallowed his spit and his mouth was drier than he had ever remembered. He was thirsty. He was thirsty for water, but he also thirsty for knowledge. He didn't understand how he had gotten there. The last thing he remembered was looking down the barrel of a gun . . . pointed by his own blood brother. He remembered hearing a shot and then everything went black. The sleeping beast had finally awoken. Monroe "Money" Diamond was alive.

Money looked around and the setting was so unfamiliar. He had no idea where he was, and his mind began to race rapidly. He had an IV hooked into his arm and patches were on his bare chest to monitor his heartbeat. Although he was under care, he noticed he wasn't in a hospital. He was in a plush, spacious bedroom that looked to be some sort of luxurious beach house, and the back French doors that led to the beach were open.

He had no idea where he was, and panic began to set in. Money felt his heart begin to speed up, and along with that the heart monitor began to beat louder and more rapidly, signaling the homecare nurse, who was in the other room. Money quickly sat up, causing him to become dizzy. He lost his balance and fell onto the floor. He tried to pick himself up, but that's when he realized how weak his limbs were.

Two Dominican nurses rushed into the room, and they were in shock as they looked at the frail, bearded man that lay on the floor. They had taken care of him while he was in a coma for years, but never had they met him personally.

The two ladies began to frantically converse in Spanish. Money picked up the accent and immediately knew that he was in the Dominican Republic. As a child, his mother would speak that language when she got angry, so he caught on quickly.

They just stared at him in shock as they placed their hands over their mouths. Monroe, being fearless and refusing to be defeated, tried to get to his feet again. Almost instantly, he crumbled to the ground, not being able to get his legs under him. The nurses rushed over to him, one of them grabbing him by each arm. He aggressively snatched away and grimaced.

"I . . . I got it," he said faintly as he clenched his jaws so tightly that veins began to pop out in his forehead. One of the nurses ordered the other one to go call Estes and notify him that his grandson had awoken.

He gathered himself and tried to get up again. This time he used the bed as a crutch as he climbed to his feet, gritting his teeth as it took all of his might and willpower. He slowly got to his feet and stood up straight and poked his chest out. He refused to be defeated, and the nurses watched as he breathed heavily. He was obviously in pain.

"Where am I?" he asked as he looked at the nurses.

Just as he finished the sentence, the nurse who had left the room returned with a phone in hand. She walked up to Money and gave it to him. He reached for the phone as he leaned on the bed to help him stay upright. He then slowly raised the phone to his ear. He just listened as he waited to hear who was on the other side of the phone.

"Monroe Diamond. Is it true?" Estes asked as he listened to Monroe breathing on the phone. It was silence in the air, and Estes wanted nothing more than to hear the sound of his favorite grandchild's voice.

"Speak to me!' Estes yelled through the phone in an attempt to confirm the news. Monroe's mouth felt like sandpaper, and he cleared his throat so that he would be clear.

"I am here, Papa. I am here," Monroe confirmed.

"I am on my way!" Estes said calmly. Estes knew that he had a tough task ahead. He had to let Monroe know that things weren't as he had left them. Taryn, his mother, had been murdered, his sister had been through hell, and his twin brother had met his fate in Brazil. "Get some rest and I'll be there immediately," Estes ordered.

"Wait, Papa. Where am I? Why am I here?" Monroe asked, trying to fill in the blanks.

"You are in the Dominican Republic at one of my private estates. You used to go there as a young boy every summer with me. Do you remember?" Estes asked.

Monroe looked around, and slowly the memories began to resurface. "Yes, Papa, I remember. But why am I all the way out here? How long have I been out?" Monroe questioned.

"Five years," said Estes.

"Wha . . . What?" Monroe said as he sat down on the bed in confusion.

"It has been five years since you slipped into the coma. A lot has changed since then. I will talk to you as soon as I get there," Estes said as his voice began to crack. He knew that telling Monroe the news would be one of the hardest things he ever had to do.

"Five years?' Monroe said almost in a whisper as he was mentally thrown into the abyss.

"Yes . . ."

Estes was on the first jet to the Dominican Republic to break the news to his grandson that he was the last male of the bloodline alive. He would tell Monroe the whole story, excluding nothing of what had happened.

***

Young Carter woke up in cold sweats as the thundering and lightning caused chaos in the sky. He sat up
from his bed, breathing deeply as he wiped the sweat
from his forehead. His bare chest was drenched as
sweat beads covered his whole body. He slowly got out
of bed and walked over to the bathroom that was connected to his room. He turned on the water and bent
down to splash water in his face.

The nightmares had haunted him every day since
he murdered Mecca. He always wished that he could
take the murder back, but when he thought deep about
it, he knew that he had to do it. Mecca's character was
flawed, and he eventually hurt the people who were
close to him. Young Carter knew he did what he had to
do.

He looked into the mirror and into his own eyes. Unlike many, he could see his soul. He was content with
the person he was. The last year had been a peaceful
one for him. He fell all the way back from the streets
and let Zyir take over. He only came into the picture
when it was time to meet with their supplier.

Carter knew that he wouldn't be able to go back to
sleep, so he slipped on a T-shirt and walked into his living room. He clicked on SportsCenter and walked over
to his mini bar to pour a glass of cognac. He needed to
take the edge off and get his mind off the murder.

The loud roars of the thunder were like a soundtrack
to a horror film, and the rain began to pour down like
cats and dogs. As he poured himself a glass, he felt a
chill go up his spine. Things weren't right.

Just as he put the glass to his lips, he heard his doorbell ring. He instantly focused his attention on the door
and frowned up. *Nobody knows about this place but*

Zyir, he thought as he walked to his room and grabbed his gun off the dresser. He tucked it in the small of his back and headed to his door. He unlocked his door, and when he saw who stood on the other side, he dropped his glass. He was seeing a ghost—he had to be, because he was looking at a person he thought was dead a long time ago. *Oh my God,* he thought as he looked into the eyes of . . .

Chapter 2

"If you can't forgive me just kill me, Carter, because I can't live without you."
—Miamor

Miamor stood before him, hair soaked as the heavens cried tears of retribution upon her. Her wet skin glistened under the glowing porch light, while her body shook from the chill that settled into her bones. Hers was a face that Carter hadn't seen in four years, but he had committed it to memory in his feeble attempts to hold on to the love that they had once shared.

Young Carter's knees weakened as his heart matched the rhythm of the lightning bolts that struck the black sky. Pain pierced his chest as heartbreak seared through his body. It was as if Cupid himself was pulling the bow out of his heart, ripping him to pieces with every tug. His eyes widened in shock as he let go of the glass of cognac he had been sipping. It shattered in a million pieces at his feet, resembling the current state of his broken heart.

There was so much history between them, and as his mind recalled their past, a myriad of emotions passed through him. Rage, hurt, and betrayal caused a lump to form in his throat as they stared silently at one another.

A pistol rested on his hip, but he didn't even think to reach for it. Had she been any other person, he would have put a bullet between her eyes, but this one woman was the exception to his street rules. Miamor had always been his weakness.

Silence surrounded them. There was so much that needed to be said, but Carter couldn't find his voice. Lost in her eyes, he saw a woman who had been through hell and back just to stand at his door. She was thinner than he remembered, and scars covered her neck and wrote imperfections onto her beautiful face.

The world seemed to move in slow motion, and Carter couldn't help but to think that he was dreaming. His mind had played this trick on him many times before. In his sleep he had held her, kissed her, made love to her, but when he awoke each morning, the loneliness of his existence always crept in. Her absence was always present. He didn't believe his eyes, despite the fact that this time he was seeing the truth.

Miamor stood, terrified as she waited for Carter to react. Butterflies fluttered in her stomach and her chest heaved up, then down, in anticipation. Her soul was bleeding out, and tears began to flow down her cheeks in turmoil. The hatred she saw in his eyes dissolved into hurt, then confusion, but behind it all she still saw love. She knew that there was a possibility that Carter would murder her where she stood, but seeing him again was worth the risk. The feeling of completion that he gave her when she was in his presence was enough to put it all on the line. She had tried staying away, but in the end living without him was not living at all.

"Please say something," she whispered as she lowered her head to her chest. For the first time she was ashamed of herself. She was so full of regret that she couldn't stomach it. Carter was always so statuesque and strong, but her reemergence had sucked the air out of his lungs. He was vulnerable, and seeing him so hurt sent a dagger through her heart.

Carter was a man of strict composure, but the melody of her voice caused him to lose it all. Tears clouded his eyes.

"This isn't real. You're dead," he whispered as he walked out onto his porch and into the heavy rain. He stepped so closely to her that there was no room between them.

Miamor's breath caught in her throat. She was afraid to breathe, afraid to move, afraid of what he was going to do to her. Certainly there was vengeance and betrayal on his heart, but she hoped that the sight of her sparked the love that they used to share. All she needed was a tiny spark to ignite a flame so great that he couldn't deny her return.

He brought his hand to her chin, lifting it so that she had to face him. His index finger traced the outline of her face as he took her in. Miamor felt the steel of his pistol pressing into her stomach, and she didn't move as she watched him weigh his options in his head—to kill her or to love her.

Carter knew that there was only one true choice. No woman could ever do for him what Miamor did for him. He had entertained plenty of playthings during her absence, but the connection that they shared was one that was only gifted by God once in a lifetime.

"Miamor," he whispered as a single tear escaped him.

His voice was like a gunshot releasing her from a racing block, giving her permission to move. She reached up to wipe his tear away.

"I'm sorry, Carter," she said.

Carter cleared his throat and took a step back from her as he grabbed her hands and removed them from his face. He moved to the side and extended his hand in welcome.

"Come inside," he said.

His voice was low, sad, and revealed a hint of disdain, but she was ready to face him. She was ready to be with him, if he would have her. She didn't need to stand before God to be judged. Reuniting with Carter Jones was her judgment day. She only hoped that he didn't send her to the executioner. She took a deep breath and walked into his home.

"There's so much I need to say to you . . ." she began. Before she could finish her sentence she felt the cold kiss of the gun as Carter entered behind her and pointed it to her skull.

Her body tensed and she closed her eyes. If she had to go, this would be the way to do it—at the hands of the man she loved. The perfect end to an imperfect existence. It was almost too poetic. "I never meant to hurt you, Carter," she said. Her voice was so full of sorrow that her words caused Carter's pulse to quicken and his jaw to clench. "I don't deserve your forgiveness. I knew that it could come to this if I came back, but I had to see you. I had to see you see me. Even after you pull that trigger, just know that I will always love you. I always have, and if I could do things over again, I would do them differently."

She waited for words, for bullets, for any type of response from him, but Carter was silent. "Carter, say something," she pleaded as she began to cry. "Tell me you love me. Say that you hate me. Just say something because the silence is torture."

Carter had never been a novice when it came to his pistol. When he drew his gun he always popped off, but Miamor was tugging at his heartstrings. He had lived for too long thinking that she was dead. He had grieved over her. Now that she had miraculously reappeared in his life, could he really be the one to make her extinct?

His heart said no, but his mind said maybe. Still no part of him was able to say yes.

His hand shook, and Miamor could feel the uncertainty in his aim. She raised her hands in defense.

"I killed Mecc . . ." Carter couldn't even finish his sentence as he closed his eyes, finally allowing his pain to release in the form of flowing tears.

"I know," she whispered. "You killed Mecca for me, and I'm sorry I put you in that position, Carter. If you hadn't done what you did, I would have spent the rest of my life running from him."

Emotions ran high as Miamor spoke and Carter's conscience weighed heavily on him. "He was my brother."

"A brother that murdered *my* sister!" she contested with emotion, her voice raising an octave in defense. The loss of Anisa was still very real to her, and Carter was picking at the scab.

She closed her eyes and composed herself, taking a deep breath. She had no right to ever raise her voice, not with Carter. He was a victim of her betrayal. She lowered her voice to just above a whisper as she continued. "That's what started it all. What was I supposed to do, Carter? I kill. That's all I've ever known." She raised her hands and looked at them; although they were clean, in her mind they were covered in blood. "I've taken more lives than I can count. It's who I am, and your brother took my sister from me. So I did what I do best, but then you happened. *We* happened."

Carter smirked sarcastically and said, "Big coincidence."

"It was, Carter," Miamor replied, breathless because her heart was beating so intensely. "I didn't mark you. Meeting you was the best thing that has ever happened to me and it was not planned. You weren't on my shit list. What we had was the realest thing I have ever known. I'm in love with you, Carter, and I need you to save me from myself," Miamor sobbed.

Carter's grip loosened around his gun as she melted his resolve for vengeance. His eyes were focused on the nape of her neck where delicate tendrils of curls lay perfectly against her skin. Anger surged through him like an electrical current, but he couldn't will himself to pull the trigger.

He lowered his gun and wrapped his arms tightly around her waist, burying his face in the crease of her neck. It was at that moment that her legs gave out as she wept. Carter lowered her to the ground and kissed the back of her neck while her sobs of regret filled the room. They both were being smacked with the reality of the mistakes that they had made.

"If you can't forgive me just kill me, Carter, because I can't live without you. I've tried and it's too hard," Miamor cried.

Carter tossed the gun out of arm's reach and held her tightly. She leaned back against his chest and allowed herself to become weak as he rocked her slightly. They sat in the middle of his extravagant foyer, clinging to each other desperately, because neither of them knew how long this moment would last. There was so much deception between them that love could transform into hate within the blink of an eye, and when it did, Miamor would have no one to blame but herself.

She felt him lift her from the floor and she buried her face in his chest as he carried her up the stairs. When they reached one of the rooms, he stopped and placed her on her feet.

"Look at me," he said, his voice steely and despondent, yet commanding.

Miamor could barely look Carter in the eyes, but upon hearing his request she lifted her head.

"Take a shower and meet me downstairs. We have a lot to talk about," he said.

Miamor nodded her head and then retreated inside the room as he walked away from the door.

Carter's head was so clouded that he didn't know if the choice he was making was right or wrong. He wasn't a man of indecision, but when it came to Miamor he was stuck. He wanted her in the worst way, but with a ruthless history like the one she possessed, how could he ever trust that he wouldn't fall into her crosshairs? Love hadn't stopped her from betraying him before. He couldn't trust her, but it didn't stop him from wanting her by his side all the same.

***

Tears stung the lids of Miamor's eyes as she stood under the steaming hot water with her head hung low. She wept, biting her bottom lip to stop her cries from being audible. Her chest heaved and her mind spun. The slightest sound caused her to jump as she pulled back the shower curtain in paranoia. She half expected for her brains to be blown out while she washed her body. A seasoned killer, Miamor knew that the most convenient place to murder someone was in a bathtub. That way all the blood and evidence could be easily washed down the drain. To her surprise no Grim Reaper stood waiting to deliver her fate.

Miamor quickly stepped out of the shower and wrapped herself in a towel. Wiping the condensation from the mirror she stared at herself. Miamor silently condemned the woman who stared back at her. She didn't deserve Carter's forgiveness. Anything less than a bullet to the head would be generous of him.

Her sixth sense told her to run, but her heart kept her still. Miamor was tired of running in the opposite direction of the love of her life. She wanted to run toward Carter—more importantly, beside him.

She wiped the tears from her red and swollen eyes, then exited the bathroom.

Warm colors decorated the large master bedroom. This was home to Carter, and she had never thought she would be welcomed into his life again. Just being in his proximity made her feel lightheaded, grateful, and terrified all at the same time. She quickly dressed, throwing on one of Carter's button-up shirts, then hesitantly made her way down the stairs to meet her fate.

Carter stood in the dining room staring into the flickering fireplace as the amber flames danced and crackled before his eyes. Although his back was to the entryway he immediately felt Miamor's presence when she entered the room. He sucked in a breath and held it for a brief second before releasing it along with the tension that burdened his shoulders. Turning toward her he stared, coldly, in confusion. Carter had been through a lot, had seen a lot, had lived a lot, and no one had ever affected him the way that she had. Her disappearance from his life had cut him deeply, but her reemergence was like salt to a bleeding wound. It burned.

"Carter," she said with a hint of desperation in her tone, and in an instant he was across the room, standing in front of her. His hand wrapped around her fragile neck, and his body weight pushed her against the wall. His powerful presence humbled her, and standing before him she felt small, like a chastised child who was awaiting punishment for a bad deed.

Miamor breathed erratically. He could snap her neck easily, take her life in a split second and get his revenge for the things that she had done. Somehow she knew he wouldn't, or rather, he couldn't.

"Carter," she repeated. She had thought of him often over the years, but had never dared to speak his name. The syllables felt odd falling from her lips. He had been a memory for so long, someone she was supposed to let go of and forget, but he was such a prevalent force in her life that she couldn't. His face haunted her dreams every night.

He caressed the side of her cheek. He was weak and vulnerable to this one woman. The street code that he lived by wasn't complex enough to analyze his current predicament. To love a woman like Miamor was dangerous, but to not love her was torture. The hate dissolved from his stare, and against his better judgment he kissed her. His full lips covered hers as their tongues did a slow, seductive tango. Carter pulled her lips into his mouth roughly, passionately, pouring his wanting into her as their bodies pressed together.

She could feel how much he missed her and she creamed her panties thinking of the way he used to slow stroke her. Miamor's heart was stuck on Carter, and there had not been another man for her after him. His shoes were too large to fill, and as his hands gripped her face she knew why. They were designed for one another. Carter couldn't kill her if he wanted to.

His hands moved south from her neck to her collarbone, discovering her breasts, and eventually finding the wetness that flowed between her thighs. His fingertips awakened her nerve endings, causing her nipples to harden and her thighs to clench together in anticipation. He groaned as his own erection swelled. He roughly lifted her off her feet and she wrapped her legs around his waist. She reached down, her fingers fumbling as she pulled at his belt and unbuckled his designer slacks. They moved with intensity; with the passion of star-crossed lovers who had been deprived of one another. Four years was a long time to be disconnected from the one you craved. Carter had an insatiable hunger that only Miamor could fulfill.

Miamor gasped and her mouth fell open in pleasure as his thickness parted her southern lips. He filled her up and made her breathless as he discovered the deep valleys of her womanhood. Miamor's brows dipped in pleasure as Carter handled her roughly, taking out his frustrations as he hit the back of her pussy. His rhythm was slow, but powerful as he fucked her deep, long-stroking her into a frenzy as she creamed around him.

"Carter," she gasped.

His mixed emotions caused him to handle her differently. He wasn't as gentle as she remembered. He was punishing her love box, and Miamor loved it as she arched her back and brought her hips forward to match his stroke. Her shoulders balanced on the wall as Carter ripped open her shirt, revealing her perky breasts. Her nipples were hard, rippled, and Carter palmed one breast, rolling her nipple gently between his thumb and index finger.

Miamor's head fell back and her eyes followed suit as they rolled in the back of her head. Ripples of ecstasy flowed through her body as Carter sexed her into an orgasm. It quaked her body from head to toe as she held him tightly.

He buried his face in the groove of her neck, planting gentle kisses on her delicate skin as he felt the blood surge to the head of his dick. She felt his nut building. The strong veins that ran through his shaft pulsated inside of her, and Miamor clenched down on him, as she wound her body slowly, grinding her sex into him.

Miamor had beaten Carter to the finish line, but she was determined to make him catch up.

Carter gripped the back of her hair and pulled her neck back slightly, taking complete control over her. Their sweaty bodies grinded harder. Faster. Harder. Miamor exploded again. She squirted all over him, and her wetness caused Carter to release. He came so far in her belly that she screamed his name and clawed at his back before finally letting the wave of ecstasy wash up on the shore.

Spent, Miamor rested against the wall as Carter leaned into her, breathing erratically, heavy as their foreheads met. He cupped her face with one hand and her knees went weak as she stared into his pained eyes.

"Forgive me," she whispered, their lips only inches apart.

Carter shook his head from side to side, closing his eyes as he memorialized Mecca in his mind. Could he possibly pardon her?

"Look at me," she said, her voice small and distressed. He did as she asked. "Forgive me, Carter." She could see the inner battle that he was fighting in his mind. To trust her or not, that was his dilemma.

He cleared his throat and stood upright as he sniffed and flicked his nose quickly, gathering himself. He adjusted his clothing and shot her a look that was filled with disappointment. He walked over to the fully stocked bar and poured himself a glass of expensive cognac. He wasn't a drinking man, and he usually gave himself strict limits. He indulged in nothing that had the ability to affect his reasoning, besides Miamor. She was his only vice, the addiction that he couldn't quite kick. But tonight he needed something to take the edge off.

He shook his head and stared at Miamor from where he stood. He scoffed slightly, thinking of everything that she had done, all the lies that she had told him. Holding his glass in his hand, he extended his pinky finger and pointed at her mockingly.

Miamor stood still as she let him go through his emotions. She was afraid to speak, because she knew that nothing she said could make things right between them. Carter brought the glass to his mouth and in one swig he downed the rest of the Louis and then tossed the crystal glass against the wall nonchalantly as he walked out of the room. Miamor flinched when it shattered into a thousand pieces against the wall. She didn't call for him. She simply stood there devastated as she thought, *He'll never look at me the way he used to.*

Defeated, she walked over to the shattered glass and began to pick up the pieces, wishing that her life were just as easy to clean up. Overwhelmed, she collapsed against the wall and cried out tears of regret. Part of her wished that she had never met Carter Jones. Then she wouldn't be so lost and stuck in such a dark place. Whoever said that it was better to have loved and lost obviously didn't know her story. To lose a love like Carter's hurt tremendously and would surely fill her days with regret as long as she lived. No one understood her plight. The game had her loyalty and she was in it to win it, but since the moment she saw Carter across a crowded casino, he seized her heart.

Suddenly, Carter reentered the room. "I want to hear it from you. I want to hear it from your lips what happened and everything that you've done. You've got to show me who you are, Miamor, because right now I have no clue," he said. He pulled out one of the dining room chairs and motioned for her to come to him. "Sit down. Tell me your story."

Miamor and Carter stayed up all night as he listened to the candid tale that was her life. She left nothing out, admitting to it all, even the death of Taryn, as she spilled her guts to him. She watched as shock, anger, and sadness filled his eyes. Certain parts enraged him while others made him sympathetic. He grilled her, asking questions that he had pondered on for years, and she answered him honestly.

It took hours for her to tell it all, but only seconds for him to decide that he loved her despite it. No one would understand the connection he had to her, but he was the boss so no one needed to. He answered to no one, and as he heard her hidden truths he realized that he couldn't pass judgment. The same way that she had taken life, he had taken life, Mecca had taken life, and his father had taken life. It was a part of the lifestyle they led. They all had their burdens to bear and their own crosses to carry. Killing his brother would weigh down his heart for the rest of his days, but he couldn't let Miamor disappear from his reach once again. The first time had crippled him. The second time would kill him. His only resolution was to forgive.

As the sun rose above the clouds, Carter reached across the table and grabbed Miamor's hand. She was emotional, frenzied, and weak as she trembled from his touch. Her red eyes met his.

"You hate me?" she asked.

"No," he replied simply. He stared into her soul and concluded that she was his. Jaded past, faults, and all, she belonged to Carter. "Can you be loyal to me?" he asked.

"I want to be loyal to you, Carter. I can be," she replied as she lowered her gaze.

"Look at me, Mia. I want you to understand what I'm asking you because should you misstep again the consequence will be severe. There will be no more room for forgiveness."

She lifted her head and witnessed a glint of the devil that hibernated inside of him.

"Yes, I can be loyal to you," she said.

He leaned in and kissed her forehead. "Then welcome home."

Chapter 3

"You're in Miami, bitch, and *mi familia
quisiera matar tu . . . lentamente.*"
—Breeze

"Look at what you did to me!" Breeze screamed as
she stood over Illiana, the woman who had almost
taken her life. Her shirt was open and a long scar ran
from her sternum to her navel. It bubbled gruesomely
and its red hue stood out against her bright skin. It was
the only imperfection on the perfectly pampered Diamond princess. It was her war wound, a reminder that
she had been involved in one of the worst street beefs
that Miami had ever seen.

"It suits you. I just wish I had cut a little deeper;
then you wouldn't be standing here right now," Illiana replied slickly as she spit at Breeze's feet. Breeze
looked down at the now ruined Giuseppe pumps.
Breeze hauled off and slapped Illiana, causing her head
to snap violently to the right. The two goons who held
Illiana in place didn't flinch as they stopped Illiana
from lunging at Breeze, restraining her by the arms.

"My family is going to kill you," Illiana said with a
sneer as she jerked against the two goons who held her
in place.

Breeze smiled mockingly and replied, "No, dear, I
think you have that the wrong way around. Let me put
this in a way you can understand. This isn't Mexico.

You're in Miami, bitch, and *mi familia quisiera matar tu . . . lentamente.*"

The threat of a slow death at the hands of The Cartel was enough to instill fear into Illiana's cold heart. Her face drained of all color as she blinked away tears. Zyir stepped up and placed a hand on the small of Breeze's back. "It's time to go. You don't need to see what's about to occur," Zyir said. He kissed the back of Breeze's neck and she turned to face him.

"Make it hurt," Breeze said. She put her Burberry glasses on her face and then walked out of the warehouse with a model's precision.

Illiana's eyes followed Breeze and her temper flared. The click-clack of Breeze's stilettos taunted her. "You bitch! You fucking bitch!" she shouted.

Zyir nodded his head to the goons as he rolled up his sleeves patiently, his face tense and focused for the upcoming task at hand. "Hoist her from the rafters, and find me a steel pipe." The goons dragged her away kicking and screaming. "And cover the floor in plastic. It's going to get messy!" Illiana had almost taken everything from Zyir, and now he was going to turn her into a human piñata. He had goons to put in this type of work, but this was a death sentence that he wanted to personally deliver.

***

The humid, salty air blew through Breeze's short hair as she whipped through the Miami streets. Little Breeze Diamond had done a lot of growing and was no longer the naïve little girl her father had once shielded from the streets. Unlike most, she had seen the other side. She knew what it felt like to die. The doctors had narrowly saved her after being stabbed up by Illiana. She had coded five times before they finally put her in a medically induced coma. She had sat at a table with her dead loved ones, but it hadn't been her time to take her seat yet. God gave her another chance at life; consequently Breeze just wanted to live. She knew that she would never be able to do that as long as Illiana breathed. The world wasn't large enough for the both of them, so when Zyir asked her what she wanted him to do about it, Breeze put in the order of extermination. *She fucked with the wrong one,* Breeze thought.

Breeze had been through too much to remain the same. Her eyes had witnessed death in too many ways and it had changed her. It made her realize the lifestyle that her father, brothers, and even her mother had led was more dangerous. They weren't living the lifestyles of the rich and famous; they were living the life of American gangsters, and she had learned the hard way to move accordingly.

Breeze's fingers lightly touched the still painful scar. It was tender to touch and it brought tears to her eyes. She was so grateful to be alive. To have had a second chance to love a man like Zyir for a lifetime humbled her. He was her everything. Nothing could ever tear her away from that man, not even an envious, conniving force like Illiana. *You lose, bitch,* Breeze thought. She pulled into the driveway of her oceanfront double villa and placed her car in park. Her head spun as she thought of all that her family had been through. Thinking of the pieces of her life that she had lost, her chest became heavy. The Diamond family had once been so close, so strong, but outside forces had come in and annihilated them. *Rest in love,* she thought. She gripped her steering wheel and lowered her head as she began to cry.

The Cartel was in transition, and Zyir was the new head of state. Breeze had just been crowned the new queen, and it excited and frightened her simultaneously. The last thing she wanted was to be someone else's target in another war, and as Zyir's wife she was vulnerable. She hoped that he would keep her protected and untouchable to the street's ills.

A knock at the window alarmed her, and she quickly wiped her eyes as she turned to see Leena holding her nephew, Monroe II, in her arms. Breeze exited her car and gave Leena a smile and quickly scooped the baby from her.

"Are you okay?" Leena asked.

Breeze nodded and replied, "Yes, I'm fine. Are you two headed out?" Breeze asked.

"Just to grab lunch. You wanna join us? It looks like you could use a sangria or two or three," Leena said with a charmingly beautiful smile.

Leena had become a part of the family. She held the only connection left to Monroe. She had borne his son and that immediately endeared her to The Cartel. She was kept and protected as if her last name were Diamond as well. Breeze even welcomed Leena into her home so that she wouldn't miss a beat of her nephew's life. The women had grown closer than close. Leena helped Breeze balance out the testosterone-heavy Cartel. She was like the sister Breeze never had.

The sound of her cell phone ringing caused her to pause. "I'll get the baby set up in the car while you take your call," Leena said.

Breeze looked down at the screen and didn't recognize the number. She immediately sent it to voicemail, but when the number called back her curiosity was piqued.

"Who is this?" she asked, knowing that only a select few had her number.

"It's your grandfather."

Breeze's breath caught in her throat at the sound of Estes's voice. She missed him dearly, but had mixed emotions toward him because of his refusal to supply Zyir and Carter. He had been the connect who kept The Cartel strong while her father reigned, but things had gone stale after her father's death. Her grandfather refused to supply The Cartel with Young Carter and Zyir as its leaders, and consequently his relationship with Breeze hadn't been the same since.

"Hello, Estes," she replied.

"I need to meet with you immediately. Come to my estate tomorrow evening at eight o'clock. It is imperative, Breeze. Do not be late."

Breeze stood there dumbfounded by the unexpected call as she heard the dial tone blare in her ear. His instructions were clear and he gave away no clues as to what she should expect. One thing for sure was that when Estes called there was usually a storm brewing. Breeze just hoped that her family could withstand whatever blow he was about to deliver.

Chapter 4

"He is dead to the world, not us."
—Estes

As Young Carter looked around the roundtable, he saw his family. Although his body was there physically, his mind was a thousand miles away. Visions of his Miamor clouded his thoughts. Her scent, her face, and the thoughts of all the deception she had been a part of. He looked around the table and saw all of the family that he had left, which were Zyir andBreeze. The sound of the French doors opening interrupted his thoughts. All eyes shot to the entryway, and the tension in the room was so thick that it could have been cut with a knife. As the remaining members of the Diamond family sat at the table, no one said a word. They all were clueless and wondering what was the cause for the meeting called by Estes.

Estes, with a walking cane in his right hand, slowly walked toward the table and took a seat at the head of it. Everyone's attention was on Estes as he pulled out a cigar and lit it, taking his time as he usually did. He slowly puffed on the Cuban until it was well lit and blew out a cloud of smoke.

"I want to thank everyone for coming this evening. I called this meeting to make an announcement. I made a very important decision a couple of years back," Estes said as he took his time with his words, enunciating every syllable. "I made a decision to keep a secret from the family and, looking around the table, I believe I made the right call," he stated.

The room was so quiet you could have heard a pin drop. Everyone was wondering what Estes was about to say. However, the anticipation would not last long. Just as the last word slipped out of Estes's mouth, in came Monroe "Money" Carter. He hadn't missed a beat. He walked in in a three-piece Armani suit with a model's posture. His face was clean shaven, just as he always kept it, displaying his strong jawbone and smooth skin.

Everyone's heart dropped as they saw the familiar face appear. Breeze let a small gasp escape as she put her hand over her lips. It was as if she had seen a ghost. She actually thought she was seeing a ghost, seeing that she had buried her brother years ago. It was too unreal to her.

Money walked directly to Breeze and she stood up. Money was slightly taller than she, and he looked down at his sister. They stared directly into each other's eyes, both not knowing what to say. What could a person say after going through what they had been through? Before Money slipped into a coma, his whole family was alive and well. Fast-forward years later . . . everyone was gone.

"Monroe," Breeze whispered as she gently cupped the right side of his face. "Oh, my God. It's really you," she said as she shook her head in disbelief. Her brother, twin of Mecca, was there in flesh. Monroe was back.

It seemed like Money had an instant flashback when he saw his sister's eyes. The horrible night that put him in the coma resurfaced to his memory when he saw his baby sister.   ***

Five Years Prior

Money drove Mecca's Lamborghini down the highway toward Leena's home. Money hated driving Mecca's cars. In his eyes they were way too flashy and drew too much attention. Money glanced over at Leena while she cried quietly, wishing she had never come out that night. Money wanted so badly to be with Leena, but he couldn't betray his brother in that way. He gently ran his hand over her cheek and wiped her teary eyes, trying to comfort her.

"Mecca doesn't mean any harm. He does love you; he just has a fucked-up temper, nah mean?"

"He sure has a fucked-up way of showing me he loves me," Leena said as tears streamed down her face and she kissed Money's hand as he rubbed her cheek.

Money thought Leena was crying because of what Mecca had just done to her, but that was the furthest thing from her mind at that point. The tears were coming from the thought of her knowing that she and Money could never be. Leena placed her hand on her stomach as she melted in Money's hand. She had found out that morning that she was three weeks pregnant with Money's child. She knew it was Money's because she hadn't been intimate with Mecca in months. He had been too busy to satisfy her lately. She decided to have an abortion and take her secret to her grave, but the pressure was too much to handle by herself; she had to tell Money.

"Money, I'm pregnant," Leena said almost in a whisper.

"What?" Money asked as he swerved in traffic, not believing what he had just heard.

"I said I'm pregnant, Money! It's your baby."

"What are you talking about? How do you know it's mine? It ain't mine. I strapped up every time!" Money expressed with skepticism in his voice.

"I know it's yours because you are the only person I have been with. Mecca and I haven't done anything in months. I know it's yours! Remember that night . . . after those niggas tried to rob Mecca?" Leena asked, referring to the last time they had made love without using protection.

Money kicked himself inside, knowing the time she was talking about. He was so caught up in the moment he slid up in her raw, and now he was paying the consequences of his actions.

"Fuck!" Money yelled as he hit the steering wheel out of frustration. The guilt began to set in as Money thought about how he had betrayed his best friend and twin brother.

✳✳✳

"I love you, Leena," Mecca whispered just before he lowered his face to his table to inhale the line of cocaine. As soon as Breeze dropped him off, his conscience began eating at him. He felt bad for putting his hands on the only woman he had ever truly loved. His long hair was wild and unbraided, which made him look like a madman as he used his nose as a suction vacuum for his preferred drug.

Mecca threw his head back and held it up to prevent his nose from running. Mecca was high out of his mind. He had snorted five grams of coke within twenty minutes, and the effects of the drugs were kicking in. He grabbed the bottle of Rémy Martin and took a large swallow of it. Mecca distantly heard a Tupac song pump out of his home stereo and recognized the tune. He stood up, almost stumbling, and went over to turn the music up. "'All I need in this world of sin is me and my girlfriend . . . Down to ride to the very end, just me and my girlfriend.'" Mecca held the bottle of Rémy in his grasp and drunkenly rapped along, thinking about his love, Leena. He couldn't take it anymore. He had to go over to Leena and make things right. His conscience was getting the best of him. Although he treated Leena bad at times, he really was in love with her and she was the only woman he had truly ever loved. Mecca staggered over to the keys to his Benz and snatched them off the counter. He was about to confess his love for Leena.

"Leena, I love you, baby. I'm sorry," he said as he stumbled out the door and into his Benz. He was about to go see his woman.

✳✳✳

"I don't know what to do, Money. I'm in love with a man I can't have," Leena said as tears streamed from her eyes. She sat on her sofa across from Money expressing how she felt about him. Their brief love affair turned into an undeniable desire to be with one another.

Money was speechless as he looked into Leena's eyes and realized the feeling was mutual. He began to slowly shake his head, knowing that what they had done was wrong. His father taught him that family always comes first and loyalty is the single most important thing a man can have for his family. Money's father's teachings were embedded in his brain as his heart and mind played tug of war. On one hand he knew that betraying his brother was wrong, but on the flipside, not taking responsibility for what he had created would eat at him. His father also told him that abortion is wrong and a real man takes care of his family by any means necessary. Money was lost.

"Leena, this ain't right. This ain't right," he mumbled as he buried his face in his palms. All Money could think about was his twin brother. Money had no other choice but to force an abortion upon Leena. He wasn't willing to let a woman come between him and his sibling.

That's my flesh and blood, my brother . . . Blood in, blood out. I can't let her have that baby, Money thought as he looked at Leena crying her eyes out. What he felt for Leena was more than just a sexual attraction; he reluctantly loved her.

Money sat next to her so that he could console her. He ran his fingers through her hair and gently put his finger under her chin and made her look at him in the eyes.

"Leena, we are going to get through this . . . together. We can't have this baby, though. It is wrong," Money said as he returned the deep stare at Leena.

"I never wanted it to be like this," Leena added, heartbroken.

"Everything is going to be okay. But this between us has to stop," Money replied as he gently kissed Leena on the lips. Money's lips were magic to Leena. Just by his touch, he drove Leena wild. She felt her friend in between her legs begin to thump, and before she knew it her hands were in his pants looking for his rod. She gently began to stroke it, to make it grow. Money promised himself this would be the last time he would have sex with his forbidden love.

✳✳✳

"'All I need in this world of sin . . .'" Mecca sang drunkenly as he approached Leena's house. He was going to apologize to his woman and make things right.

When he pulled up he noticed his Lamborghini parked in her driveway. "Money still here?" he asked himself as he pulled two houses down from Leena's house. He threw the car in park, grabbed the half empty bottle of Rémy, and hopped out. Mecca staggered to Leena's house and noticed that the front light was on. He walked in front of the house, and what he saw through the front glass made his heart drop.

Mecca dropped the Rémy bottle, causing it to shatter into pieces on the sidewalk. He saw his twin brother passionately kissing his woman and sadness overcame him. He watched as Money pulled out one of Leena's big brown breasts and began to suck on it.

Mecca was in complete shock as he watched Leena straddle his brother. His eyes bugged out as he saw his brother rub on Leena's behind with one hand while removing her thong with the other. "What the . . ." Mecca stammered as he looked in disbelief. He walked closer to the front glass and witnessed the treachery happening.

Money and Leena were so into one another that they didn't notice Mecca staring at them through the large front glass. Leena's moans could be heard from the outside as she rode Monroe with more passion than she had ever given to Mecca.

Mecca's sadness instantly turned into rage as he reached for his gun and headed for the front door. Seconds later, bullets from Mecca's .40-cal pistol were ripping through the front door wood. Leena scrambled to the corner of the room out of fear. She didn't know what was going on. Money grabbed his pistol from his waist and pointed it at the door out of instinct. He saw Mecca bursting through the front door with tears in his eyes.

"Mecca!" Leena yelled as she saw the look in his eyes. She knew that their secret was out of the bag. She had gotten caught with Money red-handed.

"I can't believe you, bitch!" Mecca screamed as he pointed his gun at Leena.

Money put away his gun and tried to calm down his brother. "Mecca, put the gun down! It's not what it looked like," Money tried to explain.

"It's not what it looked like? Nigga, fuck you!" Mecca said as he pointed his gun at his brother. Mecca's heart was broken. The two people he thought he could trust were the very ones deceiving him. Mecca pulled the hammer back on his gun and aimed it at his brother's head. Money put both of his hands up and tried to reason with his brother. Money knew his brother very well, and when he looked in Mecca's eyes, it was obvious that he was high as a kite.

"Bro, listen! Put the mu'fuckin' gun down. You high! Now stop before you do something you gon' regret," Money pleaded.

"The only thing I regret is fuckin' with this stankin' ho!" Mecca yelled as he pointed his gun back at Leena. The thought of her being intimate with his brother sent him over the edge. "I hate you!" Mecca screamed as he put both of his hands on his head. His tears began to fall freely with no shame. "I loved you," Mecca whispered just before he pointed the gun at Leena and let off two rounds. He watched as the bullets ripped through her chest and she fought for air.

"Noooo!" Money yelled as he rushed over to Leena and cradled her in his arms. "Breathe, Leena, breathe!" he instructed her as blood oozed out of her mouth. Leena fought for her dear life as she gripped Money's hands and looked into his eyes. "Breathe, Leena!" Money screamed as he tried to keep her from slipping away. "Call an ambulance!" he yelled as he looked back at his brother. Mecca was pacing the room with both of his hands on his head.

"Oh my God. What have I done?" he whispered as he frantically continued to pace the room. He looked over at his brother and Leena and what he saw and heard broke his heart. Before she lost consciousness, Leena looked Money in the eyes and whispered, "I love you, Monroe Carter."

A single tear slid down Money's face and he felt Leena's grip suddenly loosen and he knew that she was gone.

A tear fell from Mecca's eye also, but it wasn't one of sorrow, but a tear of rage. He just witnessed the woman he loved tell his brother that she loved him. "Her last words were that she loved you . . . not me," he whispered as he slowly raised his gun and pointed at Money. Money ran his hand over Leena's eyelids to close them and then he gently kissed her forehead before he turned his attention on his brother.

"Mecca, put . . . the gun . . . down," Money instructed as he put his hands in front of him.

"You always thought you were better than me, nigga! You could have had any woman you wanted, but you had to take mines. Now look at you! Look what you made me do. Look! Papa and Ma always favored you over me," Mecca cried as the tears fell freely down his face and his hand began to shake. He remembered what his parents used to say when he would get in trouble, and he began to mimic them. "You need to be more like Monroe . . . Monroe wouldn't act like that."

Mecca's voice was shaky, and Money knew his brother was unstable. As all of his emotions boiled over, Mecca looked Money in the eyes and let off a single shot that entered the left side of his chest where his heart resided. Monroe heard the gunshot, but didn't believe his own flesh and blood had shot him. As the burning sensation in Money's chest settled in, Money fell to the ground and his life slowly slipped away. High out of his mind, Mecca watched as his brother lay in a puddle of his own blood . . . dying.

***

Estes and Taryn looked at Monroe through the clear glass and watched as he struggled for his life. They had registered him under John Doe to be cautious. They were in the middle of a war and didn't want to take any chance. Estes held his daughter Taryn in his arms as she wept like a baby. To see her son on the hospital bed with tubes stuck down his mouth was very frightening.

"I already lost my husband to this war with the Haitians. I can't lose my son, Papa. Please, Lord!" she pleaded as she crumbled in his arms.

Estes hated being so powerless and wished he could change the situation, but it was in God's hands at that point. Estes wanted revenge on the Haitians badly, but at his old age he understood that he wasn't built for war.

They watched as the doctor observed him closely and exited the room. As he entered the hallway, he headed straight to Estes and Taryn.

"I have good news and bad news for you guys," the older Caucasian man said as he used his index finger to balance his glasses on the bridge of his nose. Estes took a deep breath and took a step forward. While one hand was still over Taryn's shoulder, he prepared himself for whatever the doctor would say.

"The good news is that he is going to make it," the doctor said, cutting straight to the point.

"Thank God," Taryn whispered as she put her hand on her chest in relief.

The doctor closed his eyes as if what he was about to say hurt him to say it. "However, he has slipped into a coma," he said.

"What? A coma?" Taryn asked as she felt her knees get weak and almost give out on her.

"How long?" Estes asked.

"That's something we don't know. It could be a couple hours, years, or . . . never. It all depends," the doctor said. Estes turned to his daughter and hugged her tightly.

"I can't do this anymore, Papa. I cannot lose my son," she stated as she cried inconsolably.

Estes's mind began to race. He knew that it was only the beginning of the bloodshed and heartache. He knew that the Haitians were coming for blood and would not stop until one side was completely gone. With Big Carter gone, he knew the odds were not in their favor. He, at that moment, made a decision for the sake of his bloodline.

"Monroe is dead," he said as he grabbed Taryn by both of her shoulders and looked into her eyes.

"What?" Taryn asked confused. She looked over at Monroe through the glass and saw that he was still breathing and she didn't understand what Estes was talking about.

"He is dead to the world, not us. I have to make a decision for the family and our bloodline. This has gone too far and it is only going to get worse. The Haitians *will not* stop until everyone in this family is destroyed. Monroe can't defend himself, so I have to do it for him."

Taryn looked into her father's eyes and saw him tearing up. She had never once in her life witnessed that from her father. A man who possessed so much power and so much strength had finally let his emotion seep out. Taryn knew that her father knew what was best for the family. With that being stated, she would keep Monroe's status a secret until he came to. Unfortunately, that would be the last night she would ever see her son. She died at the hands of an enemy before Money's resurrection.

✳✳✳

Present Day

"I thought you were dead," Breeze continued as a single tear slid down her face. She felt her knees tremble and she could not believe what she saw.

"I was in a coma for five years. I'm here, Breeze. I'm not going anywhere," he whispered as he fought back tears. He clenched his jaws, displaying the muscles in his jaws. He then grabbed Breeze and hugged her tightly.

He looked over at Leena, who had an expressionless face. Once his secret lover, she was now the mother of his child—a child he had no idea he had up until the previous night when Estes told him everything.

He released Breeze and headed over to Young Carter. Carter stood up and couldn't believe what he was seeing. Monroe embraced his only brother and hugged him tightly.

"I can't believe this," Carter said as he embraced Monroe.

"I can't either, bro," Monroe said. They unlocked their embrace and Carter immediately began to look into a man who resembled Mecca so closely. It was like he was seeing two ghosts in one person.

"How? I thought you were dead. I went to your funeral," Carter asked, trying to make sense of the situation.

"He wasn't dead while in that casket. You would be surprised of the things people overlook while in a church. Like, is the body still breathing while in a casket? People assume that everything in a church is the truth. This made the deception fairly easy," Estes interjected. The explanation began to unravel and everyone in the room was astonished.

"We have to move forward. Enough about the past," Monroe said as he straightened up his tie and had a look of braveness on his face. He showed no emotion at all and his backbone was as straight as an arrow. He was wearing the last name of Diamond with pride just as his father had taught him.

"A lot of things have changed while you were away," Breeze said as she dropped her head, thinking about the death of her mother and brother Mecca. "I have something to tell you," Breeze continued with water in her eyes. A tear was on the verge of dropping as she took a deep breath and closed her eyes.

"Breeze, I already know everything. Papa already told me everything there is to know. However, I have to stay strong for the family; just like Father taught me," Monroe said without a flinch. He had mourned in solitude and promised himself to stay strong for Breeze and carry on The Cartel legacy with a straight back just as his father did.

Young Carter listened closely as he watched his brother display courage and strength. Monroe just dismissed the fact that his twin brother and mother had been murdered, and he was ready to jump back into the family business. Young Carter began to grow butterflies in his stomach, realizing that he would one day have to tell Monroe that he was responsible for Mecca's death. Nevertheless, now wasn't the time, and he was glad to have his brother back.

"Welcome back, bro. Welcome back," Carter said as he looked into the eyes of his only blood brother left. Monroe returned the gesture with a nod and charismatic wink. Monroe was back.

Chapter 5

"It's amazing how many peer into a casket but never check to see if the person inside is breathing."

—Monroe

Monroe's hands gripped the steering wheel of Carter's BMW 745 as he made his way across town. Life seemed surreal now that he was home and reunited with his fractured family. The streets had most definitely changed, and Monroe was slowly realizing that taking over his family's empire wouldn't be as simple as he had anticipated. His entitlement to his father's empire was being ignored, and Monroe knew that it would be a battle to regain his position within his own family. He would have to go get his spot, but in the meantime he would have to make some power moves independently.

He had some old business to attend to. His life had been left hanging in the air, but now that he was back it was time to settle his affairs. It was apparent that life had moved on without him and that he had missed a lot in the time that he was gone. What should have been handed down to him was placed in Zyir's lap, and Money felt slighted. Zyir wasn't blood. He had no right to the kingdom that his father had built from the ground up. Money wasn't into beef, but he fully intended on taking over The Cartel. It was his destiny to head the infamous dynasty, and no matter who stood in the way he would take his place as king of Miami. It was only a matter of time.

Jamison Wildes was the most respected accountant in all of Miami. Money man to the stars, he was known for keeping everyone out of the crosshairs of the IRS. From kingpins to ball players and entertainers, his clientele were the elite of South Beach. If you were in the seven-figure gentleman's club, then you were smart enough to be a client of Jamison Wildes.

Money had been groomed for business ever since he was a young boy. He had a knack for the money flip, and his father had made sure he taught Monroe the value of a dollar. Niggas hadn't shortened his name to Money for nothing. He was about his paper, and there was a large sum left unclaimed when he had disappeared that he had to retrieve. He walked into the high-rise building and took the elevator to the top floor where the penthouse office suite sat overlooking the ocean. Jamison's company occupied the entire floor, making up an impressive modern space.

When Money entered, his presence easily overpowered the room. The Italian designer suit was tailored to his medium build perfectly, and he adjusted his slim tie as he stepped toward the receptionist.

The young woman's eyes dissected him as he approached. His handsome face and penetrating stare had her dumbfounded as she struggled to find the words to greet him.

"Umm . . . hi . . . um, do you have an appointment?" she asked.

Monroe shot the girl a charming smile and thumbed the bridge of his nose arrogantly as he said, "No, but let Jamison know that Monroe Diamond is here to see him."

The girl picked up her phone and paged Jamison's line, delivering Money's message. She frowned in confusion and put her hand over the receiver.

"I'm sorry, what's your name again? There seems to be some kind of confusion," she said.

"Tell Jamison there's no confusion. My name is Monroe Diamond," he answered.

The girl removed her hand and said, "He says he's Monroe Diamond." Moments later she hung up the phone, giving him an uncomfortable smile and reported, "He'll be right with you."

A flustered Jamison emerged from the back. "Vanessa, there has to be a mistake. Monroe Diamond is—"

"Very much alive and well," Monroe finished as he stood to his feet and extended his hand to his accountant. Jamison's eyes widened in shock and his face turned pale. "What's wrong, old friend? You look as if you've seen a ghost."

Jamison finally accepted Monroe's hand and shook it firmly. "Monroe. Forgive me, I thought . . ."

"Let's step into your office," Monroe said, taking control of the situation. "Vanessa, clear Jamison's schedule for the rest of the day. We have some business to discuss."

Monroe entered Jamison's office and walked behind the desk to take in the beautiful ocean view. Shades of turquoise and blue filled his vision as he admired the scene. "I see business is good," Monroe commented.

"I thought you were dead. I came to the funeral. How?" Jamison stammered as he watched Monroe take a seat behind his desk. Jamison sat in the visitor's chair completely thrown by the ghost of yesterday's past that had just reentered his life.

"The funeral was an illusion to trick the enemy and keep me safe. It's amazing how many peer into a casket but never check to see if the person inside is breathing," Monroe stated. "I'm not here to talk about that. I'm here for my money." He leaned in and folded his hands across the Brazilian wood desk.

"The money is unavailable," Jamison said timidly.

"Unavailable? My five million dollars that I put in your hands is unavailable?" Monroe asked. His voice was so cold that it froze Jamison in his seat. He dared not to blink or move. He could see the anger burning in Monroe's eyes.

"I . . . I . . . thought you were dead. The money was just sitting there . . ."

"Sitting there?" Monroe questioned. "So instead of taking my money to my grieving mother you did what with it?"

"I . . . I invested . . ."

Money's eyes turned dark. "You invested my dough?"

"There is a new pharmaceutical company that has created a new drug. It's not FDA approved yet, but it's only a matter of time before it happens. The money is tied up in its stock. When the FDA approval comes through I could turn five million dollars into fifty overnight," Jamison explained nervously.

Monroe was slightly irritated that Jamison had tied up his money without his permission, but he had to admit that it was a move that he would have made himself if given the opportunity. If things went according to plan the flip on Jamison's investment would be crazy. The potential gain didn't help his current financial state, however. Monroe wasn't for playing the little nigga in Carter's camp. He didn't need anyone trying to son him with handouts. He needed cash now.

"Open the account to your business," Monroe instructed.

"Excuse me?" Jamison asked. "Monroe, I don't think my company's earnings has anything to do—"

Monroe leaned back and opened his suit jacket, giving Jamison a slight glimpse of the 9 mm he had holstered underneath. Jamison began to sweat as his body temperature rose.

"You can bring me into your business, or I can focus on how you've mishandled mine," Monroe said calmly.

Jamison stood and rubbed his goatee as he walked around to the computer. He opened up his personal files, and Monroe was pleased to see that business was flourishing. Jamison was bringing in more than three million per year and had a business line of credit worth seven figures.

"Until I have that fifty million in my hands, you've got a new business partner and the split is sixty-forty," Monroe said. "Is that a problem for you?"

Jamison shook his head. Monroe stood and checked the Presidential on his wrist. "I've got to go. I'm glad we could work this out peacefully. I'll expect my name to be added on all the accounts by morning, and clear this office. It's mine now. Let this be a lesson to you, Jamison. The next time you won't touch what doesn't belong to you."

Monroe exited, and Jamison breathed a sigh of relief, letting out a slight whimper. He knew that things could have ended very badly for him. Sacrificing a piece of his business was a minor punishment in the grand scheme of things.

✳✳✳

Standing at the site where her loved ones were buried caused Breeze to tremble as tears glided down her cheeks. She stood in the land of the dead. The cemetery always seemed so cold. Even if the sun was out, a coldness always overcame Breeze when she visited the resting place of her loved ones. As she stood in front of her parents' tombstones, a cold chill ran up her spine. She was so grateful for her life and so very happy to be reunited with Monroe. Her father, her mother, and Mecca lay side by side, resting eternally. She wished that she had come from a normal family, with a blue-collar pops and a hardworking housewife. Being the child of the first family in the streets had its perks, but the downside was much worse. The violence that came with the title made Breeze yearn for regularity. "I miss you all," she said.

Breeze turned around when she heard a car door close and smiled warmly when she saw her brother's face. He approached her, and Breeze reached up to touch his face. "I can't believe you're back," she said. "I love you so much, Money. I'm so sorry you had to come back to nothing. Things got really bad after Papa died."

"How did Carter let this happen?" Monroe asked.

"The war with the Haitians crippled us, Money. There wasn't much any of us could do," Breeze whispered. Ma'tee's face flashed in her mind and sent a shiver down her spine. She quickly shook the bad memory from her thoughts as she continued. "I come here sometimes just to talk to them. I feel like they can hear me. I almost died and I saw them. I saw you too. We were sitting at a table, all of us: me, you, Papa, Mama, Mecca. . . . We were happy. We were in . . ."

"Paradise," Money finished. He knew exactly what she had seen, because he had seen it too. He was sure that there was life after death and that his family was waiting for him on the other side.

Breeze looked at him and nodded as emotion overtook her. She sniffled as she wiped her tears. "Yeah. They're in paradise. They're watching over us, Money,"

Breeze said. "There is so much hurt in our past, now I want to bring you some joy. I want to introduce you to your future."

"You're talking in circles, Breeze," Monroe said as he kissed her forehead.

"It'll all make sense soon. There's something you need to know."

✳✳✳

Leena fidgeted nervously in the mirror as her son played at her feet. Butterflies danced in her stomach. She had so many questions that she wanted to ask, but her brain didn't work at the moment. A ball of tension and nerves, she tried to calm herself, but there was no use. She was about to see the man she loved, the twin who had stolen her heart from the very first time she met him. Their situation had always been messy. She was Mecca's girl, but now things had changed. Mecca was gone and Leena bore Monroe's son. A son he didn't even know existed. *What if he doesn't want me?* she asked herself. She gripped the edge of the vanity and lowered her head. *God, please let him want me . . . let him want us.*

A knock at the door forced her to gain her composure, and she inhaled deeply than exhaled slowly. "Come in," she said.

Zyir cracked open the door, and her son jumped up to run to him. Zyir's exterior was so serious and focused, but when he interacted with Baby Monroe he always softened. Leena was grateful for men like Zyir and Carter. They had been the only male figures her son had known, and they took their roles in his life very seriously. "They're here," Zyir announced.

Leena nodded and ran her hands over her dress then made her way to the door. She grabbed her son from

Zyir, and he gave her a reassuring nod as she walked by, headed to meet her long-lost love.

She saw him before he ever knew he had an audience. He stood just as powerful as she remembered, with his shoulders squared, hands tucked into his designer slacks as he waited patiently in the foyer. By the time he noticed her, tears were flowing down her face.

"Leena," he whispered as she descended the steps. His heart fluttered from her presence, but even in his brother's death he still felt guilt from the fact that she used to belong to Mecca.

"Hello, Money," she said. His eyes drifted to the little boy she held in her arms. She adjusted her son so that Monroe could see his face. "I'd like you to meet your son."

Breeze and Zyir stood off to the side, holding on to each other as they watched Monroe's hard persona break down.

"My son?" he repeated. His brow creased as he examined the child. He immediately knew her words were true. He was staring at a mini version of himself. The little boy was the spitting image of his father, and Monroe ran his hand down his face, overwhelmed. He truly was being given a second chance at life. Yes, he had lost so much, but with the birth of one little person he felt restored. A son was more than he deserved.

He took the little boy into his arms and held on to him tightly as he fought the emotion that was threatening to spill out of him. He couldn't imagine how hard her life had been in the time he had been gone. She had buried him and had still chosen to keep his seed knowing that he would never be able to help raise him. His love and appreciation for her doubled in that moment. She was a good woman, a woman he deserved. He pulled Leena close and whispered in her ear, "Thank you."

"I can't believe that you're here. I prayed for God to bring you back to me so many times," Leena whispered.

"I haven't always done right by you, Leena, and for that I'm sorry," he said. Monroe could see years of insecurity and hurt in Leena as she stared into his eyes. He had put those things on her heart by forcing her to keep their relationship a secret. In an attempt to spare his brother's feelings he had destroyed hers, and yet she still kept his child when she could have easily gotten rid of any memory of him. When the world had put him to rest, Leena kept him alive by giving him the greatest gift . . . a son to continue his name.

"My son," Monroe whispered in awe as he kissed his mini replica on the cheek. He was in a state of disbelief, but his heart had never felt so full. He wondered if his own father had felt the same way when he had first laid eyes on his own children.

"Pack your things. I'll be back to get you and my son tonight," Monroe said.

"I feel like when you walk out that door you'll disappear again," Leena said as she lowered her head and gasped in emotional turmoil. She knew that there was no guarantee that Monroe would end up with her, but she needed him to take charge in her son's life. A boy needed his father, and she would fight for the chance for her son to know his.

"There is nothing on this earth that can stop me from coming back for you. I just have to make a few arrangements. I'll be back before you can even miss me, ma," Monroe assured.

Leena nodded and then took her baby from him before ascending the steps.

Monroe gathered himself and then turned toward Breeze and Zyir. "Thank you, Breeze, for keeping her close and taking care of my son when I couldn't," Monroe said.

"Of course, Money. She is a part of this family now," Breeze replied.

"We wouldn't have had it any other way," Zyir spoke up.

Monroe turned toward Zyir, and his face soured in contempt. He gave Zyir a cold stare but didn't acknowledge him with words. The tension placed an uncomfortable aura over the room, and Monroe scoffed and sucked his teeth in irritation as he walked past Zyir and out of the house.

His distaste for Zyir was evident, and had he been any other nigga, Zyir would have bodied him for the disrespect. Zyir tightened his jaw, reminding himself that Monroe was his brother by law. He would have to use patience when dealing with Monroe.

"He's been through a lot, Zyir," Breeze said as she rubbed her husband's face. "Give him some time to come around. Our father didn't like outsiders, and to him you're a new face."

Zyir could see the concern on his wife's face, and he kissed her lips tenderly. "Don't worry yourself, baby girl. We're all on the same team," he said. The words were true, but he knew that Monroe didn't see it as such and treachery from within was not an option. Zyir would cut the cancer out before he ever let it spread. He just hoped that it didn't come to that. He made a mental note to place a phone call to Carter, to see if he could bring his newly revived brother into the fold.

✳✳✳

The smell of new leather permeated Monroe's senses as he pushed his brand new Maserati off of the lot. He spared no expense when it came to the whips he

pushed. He enjoyed the feel of the engine as it leapt
underneath the hood while he pressed his feet on the
brake, gunning the gas simultaneously. The car leapt
as if it were a pit bull on a leash as Monroe floored his
new toy.

He checked his rearview mirror and saw that Carter
followed him in the brand new Mercedes GL he had
copped for Leena as well. Monroe was determined to
establish a new life, an affluent life for his family, and
Leena was a permanent part of his world now. A car
and a home were the least he could provide for her.
With the help of Carter's realtor, Francesca, Monroe
had found a steal on a property in a posh, secluded
neighborhood of Coral Gables and a condo in Aventura.
He could never have too much real estate. He would
put Leena up in the large estate and use the condo
whenever he needed to be closer to the action of the
city.

He pulled into his new home, opening the security
gate, and drove down the long driveway until he was finally in front of the massive mansion. Carter pulled up
behind him and got out of the car, approaching Money
as he looked around.

"Leena's going to love this, Money. I'm proud of
you, bro. This was a good choice for your family. It's
damn near perfect," Carter said as he admired the
lush greenery and elaborate fountain that sat in the
center of the circular driveway.

"I've got to pipe it out with security. Cameras,
motion sensors, a guard at the front gate, the whole
nine. I'm not sparing any expense on Leena and
Monroe Jr.'s safety," Monroe said. He was jumping
headfirst back into the streets, which meant his family would be a constant target. He was aware that
they were his only vulnerability. A smart man would

remain single and bear no children. A hustler with nothing to lose was the only one who could win in a concrete jungle.

"I've got a guy who can help you out. I'll have him give you a call," Carter offered.

The men circled the property to check out all of the exterior features of the home. "My father made sure that I grew up in a house like this. Grand, magnificent, and most of all safe. I had no worries as a child. I want the same for my son."

"This is the first step and despite what you may think, you don't have to protect him alone," Carter replied. "Your family is my family and is Zyir's family. He has uncles who love and care about him. So in the event that something happens to you, your family will always be protected."

"No offense, Carter, but Zyir is your man. I don't know him like that," Monroe said. "I don't extend the same amount of confidence in him as you do."

Carter stopped walking. "I want to make sure that you and Zyir iron out whatever differences you have. He is my brother, Monroe, as are you, and that means you two are linked by a common thread. You just have to get used to there being someone new inside of your circle. Don't worry. Zyir has passed my tests of loyalty time and time again. He will pass yours too, I'm sure," Carter replied. Monroe didn't respond as he drifted deep into his thoughts. Carter patted his brother's back and said, "Trust me, Money."

Monroe nodded and slapped hands with Carter, embracing him before they went their separate ways.

✳✳✳

"Where are we going?" Leena asked as she sat shotgun next to Monroe.

"Just sit back and enjoy the ride, Lee," Monroe responded as he steered the car with one hand and held her hand with the other.

Leena admired Monroe, watching him as he nodded his head to Jay-Z's classic anthem, "Can I Live."

They drove forty-five minutes out of the city until they pulled up to her soon-to-be residence. Monroe entered a code into the keypad and the gate opened, allowing them access.

"Whose house is this?" Leena asked as they pulled up to the front entrance.

Monroe got out of the car as Leena looked around and watched him walk around the car to her door. He opened it and held out his hand. Reluctantly, she took it.

"This is your house, a place where you and my son can always call home," Monroe said.

Leena's hand shot to her mouth, covering it in shock. "This is not my home. This house is mine?" she shrieked in disbelief as her eyes scanned the massive gift.

Monroe removed a key chain and held it up for her. "It's yours, Leena, and so is that."

He pointed the key to the Benz that sat in front of the attached garage, and Leena couldn't contain her happiness. She actually laughed because a smile wasn't enough to express how much joy she felt. For so long she had depended on others to take care of her. First Estes, then Breeze and Zyir. She was always dependent on someone else, and she never had a place to call home. Now Monroe was offering her something that was hers, something that she could decorate, something that she ruled. He had given her a kingdom of her own to do with what she pleased.

"So what does this mean for us?" she asked.

"It means that I want to take care of the ones that I care for. Things have always been complicated between us. You understand more than anyone else the sense of loyalty that I had for Mecca. Death doesn't erase that. I still feel like loving you is wrong," Monroe admitted.

Leena lowered her head and shook her head at the statement. Just like that Monroe had taken her into her past. Her past of being torn between two brothers, loving them both but wanting one more. They had been like night and day.

"Just because it's not right doesn't make it wrong, Money. I loved both you and Mecca. I was in love with you and your brother too. Mecca and I had a thing. We tried to make it work after you died. He helped me with Monroe. He was there when I needed him, and I loved him because he understood that I loved you too. He accepted the fact that I was, am, will always be torn between two great men. When I look at our son, I see you both.

Mecca was high the night that he caught us. He wasn't in his right state of mind, Money. He would have never sent bullets flying our way if he had been. He loved me, yes, and I loved Mecca. He will always have a place in my heart, but nothing can ever compare to the way I felt when I was with you. I can tell you that love has no rules, Monroe. It isn't so black and white," Leena said.

Monroe nodded his head. "It's gray," he responded as he kissed her lips.

Leena pulled away and peered up at him. "I won't love you, Mecca, or anyone else in secret, Money. I've been down that road and I won't do it again. I love you and I want *you*. I want you to live here with me and to raise our son *with* me."

Monroe stepped back from her and put his hands in his pockets. "You don't know what you want, Leena. You say you had this do-over with Mecca . . . that you loved him and he accepted your faults. Well, let me ask you, Lee. If Mecca was still alive, which one of us would you choose?" he asked.

Leena's chest heaved as her stomach knotted. There was the fated question. Which brother did she love more? This was the showdown that had been postponed for years. They were airing out all of their issues—issues that had put tension between them since day one. Tears filled her eyes but she didn't let one fall.

"I've always chosen you. You just never had the courage to choose me back. You wanted me to be a private affair. You had me in the streets strutting on Mecca's arm, but you were the one in between my legs at night! Do you know how that made me feel, Money? I felt like a plaything, like your whore," Leena shot back.

Monroe looked at her in exasperation. "You were never my whore, Leena. You were the classiest chick I'd ever met. The only one fiery enough to handle my hotheaded brother, but the only one beautiful enough both inside and out to intrigue me. Mecca needed you more than I did. That's why I never wanted you to leave him. You made my brother better! You made him happy! He just didn't know how to show you, but he always told me! My whore? Nah, you weren't my whore, Leena. You were the love of my life, ma," Monroe said.

"But I never felt that you would truly choose me over Mecca. The two of you together weren't perfect, but on the off day when you were, the entire city saw how you both shined. On those days, jealousy ate me up inside. You were his bitch, Leena. You never would have chosen me. You asked me to tell Mecca about us, but you were asking for something that you didn't really want. If you wanted it then you would have stopped fucking with Mecca on your own. You chose him."

"I wanted you!" Leena snapped, feeling angry, overwhelmed, and vulnerable all at once.

"Then prove it," Monroe said, his voice calming.

He pulled a black satin box out of his pocket and got down on one knee.

Leena's eyes widened in surprise as her tears now made a trail down her cheeks.

"Marry me," he said.

Leena was speechless as she got on her knees in front of him and clasped his wrists as she looked at the flawless, princess-cut diamond and platinum ring.

"Really?" she asked in disbelief.

"You would make me a very happy man, ma," Monroe replied with a charming crooked smile.

Leena nodded her head as she smiled happily. "Yes. Monroe Diamond, I will marry you."

Chapter 6

"You need to leave Miami. Disappear.
If you don't, the next time we cross paths
I will cut your fucking head off."
—A ghost from her past . . . Mecca Diamond

Miamor closed her eyes and retreated inside of herself as her body endured the brutal beating Fabian put
on her. Physically she was present, but her mind was
a million miles away. Detached from the reality that
loomed over her, Miamor no longer felt the pain. Each
blow was absorbed into a woman who was mentally
and emotionally drained.

This had been her entire life. Death. Destruction.
She was a terrorist and out of all her years on this
earth, she had never known true happiness. A killer
by nature, she had been so focused on revenge, on
efficiency, on the money, that she had never truly
lived. Miamor was well acquainted with death and
the ills of the world, but she knew nothing about life.

Fueled by her thirst for revenge, she had hunted
Mecca relentlessly, but as she sat looking into his eyes,
she couldn't help but wonder if it was all worth it. In
this final moment it all felt so pointless. In a normal
life he was supposed to be the brother of her future
husband. They were supposed to be connected by a
man they both loved dearly, but her existence was far

from normal. Her world was not so black and white, but instead a shade of gray where nothing made sense to her but green and red . . . money and blood.

Miamor's head hung low as her chin hit her chest. Visions of Young Carter filled her mind as her soul slipped slowly away. Her heart ached of sorrow as she remembered his smile, his confidence, his energy. She recalled how it felt to fall head over heels for his undeniable charm. It was his face that kept her mind strong as her body began to fail her.

Miamor knew that if she let Mecca into her head then she conceded defeat. He could beat her until no breath flowed through her body, but he would never conquer her mentally; she wouldn't allow it.

Her cunning wit was what separated her from the average chick. She had always been able to outthink those around her. Prideful and ruthless, Miamor couldn't be conquered, but Mecca was determined to make her break. With every vicious blow that Fabian dealt, she forced herself to take it. Her body was painted in red as if Basquiat himself had used her as his canvas. Blood flowed from her wounds like water as the irony of her impending death haunted her.

Mecca stood in the background watching intensely as Miamor was tortured slowly. The average man would have given into the pain by now, but Mecca could see in Miamor's eyes that she would not give up her life easily. She didn't want a quick death. She wanted to feel until she couldn't feel anymore.

For the first time ever, Miamor was realizing how valuable life was. She was saddened that her value had been wasted. The way that she had led her life would not earn her a spot in paradise. Her eternity would be spent in hell, and it was a fate that she feared.

A tiny voice inside of her told her to beg, plead, and bargain for her life, but the killer she had become wouldn't allow it. She was overdosed on pride and refused to ruin the hood legacy that she had built by dying on her knees. She had lived by a code that only a murderer could understand. When the streets recounted her story, she wanted them to speak the truth. She was ruthless and calculating, even when staring into the eyes of the Grim Reaper. No one, not even Mecca Diamond, had been able to break her. Miamor was the greatest to ever do it, and she refused to let Mecca take away her power.

"You fucking heartless bitch," Fabian seethed through gritted teeth as he pulled her head back. She felt the cold kiss of the gun as it met the back of her skull, and tears involuntarily welled in her eyes. Fabian's finger danced on the trigger. There weren't many people who could kill without remorse. It was a specialty that Miamor and Mecca had perfected.

"Put the bitch down and get it over with. I'm bored with this shit," Mecca stated, his voice sending chills of hatred up and down Miamor's spine. "Fuck you waiting for, nigga?"

Fabian looked up at Mecca, the unsteady grip on his pistol giving away his uncertainty as his hand shook slightly.

"You still scared of this bitch? She's tied up and you the one with the gun, but she still got you shook? Pull the fucking trigger!" Mecca ordered, shaking his head in disgust.

Fabian stood, his lean torso shaking as his bottom lip trembled in uncertainty. "I . . . I . . . can't," he admitted.

BOOM!

Without warning, Mecca sent a bullet through Miamor's shoulder.

"Aghh!"

"Fuck you mean you can't?" Mecca barked at Fabian. "See, it's simple."

BOOM!

With precision he sent another shot in Miamor's direction, this time hitting her midsection.

"Aghh!" she howled through gritted teeth as she balled her fists tightly. The bullet ripped through her organs, making it feel as though she were on fire.

Fabian backpedaled until his heel hit the bottom step of the basement. He was in over his head. Fabian dabbled in the streets every now and then, but he wasn't major. He had never led the lifestyle that Mecca had and knew nothing about this heartless side of the game. Revenge had sounded so sweet, but when it came down to it, Fabian couldn't put in the work. As Miamor gasped for air, Fabian shook his head back and forth. Jailhouse blues filled his soul as he became overwhelmed by the possible consequences of his actions. Suddenly, he wanted no part of this murderous plot.

Mecca turned toward Fabian and before he even realized it, Fabian was hightailing it up the steps.

Mecca smirked as he saw Fabian run out of the basement. "Pussy-ass nigga," Mecca scoffed, making a mental note to handle Fabian later. Mecca didn't leave loose ends. Fabian was a liability, and it was imperative that he was removed from the equation. Mecca was leaving zero witnesses, but first Mecca was going to enjoy his final round with Miamor.

"Now that there are no cowards in the room, the real fun can begin," he taunted.

Mecca grabbed the metal chain off the floor and circled Miamor. The chain scratched the floor like nails on a chalkboard, causing the hairs on the back of her neck to stand. Mecca examined Miamor as she struggled to lift her head. Her eyes followed him back and forth as he paced the concrete floor. He stopped and knelt directly in front of her, waiting to see the fear creep into her eyes. But when he stared at her all he saw was acceptance and regret.

He wrapped the thick chain around her neck. His heart beat furiously inside of his chest as he thought of avenging the death of his mother. He had waited so long for this moment that it made his dick hard.

Miamor was like a rare specimen. The Cartel had warred with a thousand armies before her, but somehow she had been able to dismantle their entire operation. One woman had annihilated his entire family. The empire that the Diamond family had built was standing on its last leg. She had destroyed the infamous Miami Cartel. Mecca hated her existence yet envied her efficiency all at the same time. She was thorough and conniving, professional and about her paper. No mark had ever been too big to hit. If the money was right, then she had no problem making it rain bullets. No questions asked. She was the Grim Reaper.

Mecca lived by the gun and knew that one day he would die by it as well. As he looked at Miamor he realized that she lived by the same creed. If he had been half as calculating as Miamor, his family would not be lined up in metal coffins under the dirt.

Since the death of his father, Mecca and Miamor had played a deadly game of cat and mouse. There was no prey among them; they were both predators. With no sheep to slaughter they had gone at each other's throats and it all culminated in this one moment. He pitied the fool who looked at Miamor and underestimated her. Her pretty face had hidden the ugliest of intentions, and it was only by God's grace that Mecca hadn't ended up on the other side of her gun.

They stared at one another silently and for a brief moment they came to a mutual understanding.

"Just do it," she whispered as tears finally came to her. "If anybody had to do it, it may as well be you. You're just like me."

Her words connected with Mecca, digging a hole straight to his heart as he nodded his head. Miamor was tired of fighting him, tired of feeling guilty for being the way that she was. She was ready for this to end.

"Tell Carter I'm sorry," she whispered, barely audible.

Mecca pulled the ends of the chain, cutting off Miamor's oxygen supply instantly. He pulled so hard that the metal pierced her skin, causing it to become raw as her eyes bulged in distress. Mecca gritted his teeth as he stared at her while choking her to death. The light in her eyes began to dwindle and the sounds around her became muffled as a natural reaction to fight overcame her. Her body jerked violently as her lungs begged for air. The tighter he pulled, the more her body rebelled, but she was helplessly bound to the chair. All she could do was die.

"Aghh!" Mecca roared as he pulled tighter and tighter on the chain. You're just like me. *Her words replayed in his head, taunting him and reminding him of the evil that lived inside of them both. Mecca stared into her face with anger, with resentment, but when he saw his own face staring back at him he froze.*

Sympathy poured into his heart as his chest became heavy.

She's right, *he thought as he backpedaled and put distance between them. Taken aback by the naked truth, he realized that as much as he hated Miamor, he couldn't condemn her. He was not without sin.*

Her lungs felt like they were on fire as she coughed uncontrollably and sucked in as much air as she could.

Mecca felt as if he were going insane. For so long he had dreamt of this very day. He had never hesitated to make an example out of a mu'fucka, but with Miamor it was different. Killing her would be like killing himself. They were the same. They both had blood on their hands, and their hate for one another kept them teetering on the edge of insanity.

"Just do it," she said with no more fight left in her voice.

A moment of clarity passed over Mecca as he turned away from her and placed his hands on his head in distress. Something bigger then Mecca's conscience was coming into play. The universe was intervening. It wasn't in God's plans for Miamor to die. Not by Mecca's doing.

"I can't," he whispered as he lowered his hands to his side and allowed the chain to fall to the ground.

Miamor was barely conscious as she craned her head to the side and replied, "What?" The blood that fell into her line of sight clouded her vision, and she was so close to giving up that she knew she couldn't have heard Mecca correctly.

"I am you," Mecca whispered with sorrow as his own tears came to his eyes. He quickly pinched the bridge of his nose and shook the emotion away. Mecca was evolving right before Miamor's eyes, and she

was so close to death that she was missing the sight. "I should fucking kill you. You deserve to die," Mecca stated, larcenous venom lacing his tone. "But something in me won't allow me to. You need to leave town and stay the fuck away from my family."

Miamor's eyes opened and closed weakly as silent tears flooded down her face.

"Don't contact Carter. Don't even enter the city limits. You need to leave Miami. Disappear. If you don't, the next time we cross paths I will cut your fucking head off," Mecca raged.

Miamor wept as his words pierced her ears. She had never felt more connected to anyone in her life. Mecca was her adversary, but today he chose to be her savior. If he could put his prideful vengeance aside and leave her with air in her lungs, then he deserved to see her break.

Miamor lifted her head, her neck bobbling loosely as she felt every broken bone in her body. "I . . . I'm sorry," she whispered.

Mecca stared at her in hatred while forcing himself to remain composed. "Disappear," he stated with finality. "Leave and never look back."

He was instructing her to do the very thing that he had wished he could do. He was pardoning her and forcing her to start over. All she had to do was pick a place and act as though a girl named Miamor had never existed. Mecca turned and walked up the steps with an agonizing ache in his heart, but a lighter soul. His mind was telling him to put a hollow tip through Miamor's chest, but his spirit was teaching him the hard lesson of forgiveness. He never looked back as he left Miamor. He was afraid that his rage might change his mind if he ever saw her face again.

Miamor waited until she was sure that Mecca had gone before she lost all composure. The cry that erupted from her battered body reflected years of pain. No one knew the things that she had suppressed, but deep inside she knew that Mecca understood. He did her no favors. She was still bound and beaten near extinction, but he had left her with a tiny chance to survive. He owed her nothing, so that tiny act was a gift. It was ironically the kindest thing that anyone had ever done for her.

Miamor grunted in excruciating pain as she used her body weight to tip the chair on its side. She wasn't ready to meet her Maker, and the only thing stopping her from surviving was the rope that bound her. She pulled with all of her might, but the beating she had endured had robbed her of her strength. She was too weak to break free, and as she twisted her wrists, the friction burned into her skin.

"Aghh!" she screamed out in frustration before finally giving up. The room spun around her as she lapsed in and out of consciousness. "God forgive me," were the last words to escape her crusted lips before everything faded to black.

✳✳✳

Miamor's eyes opened slowly and her heartbeat rapidly increased as she awakened from her four-day slumber. She was on full alert as her senses kicked into full gear. Her eyes darted around the foreign room, disoriented and confused. The sterile smell invaded her nose, making her ill instantly. It was so dark that all she could see was the fluorescent light that shined in the hallway, outlining the door to her room. Her pain was so great that it was immeasurable. Bruised and battered, Miamor was beyond repair. What she needed most was time for her body and mind to recuperate from the trauma she had endured.

How did I get here? she thought as she lay deathly still. *I have to get out of here. If Mecca finds me . . .*

The steady tone of the heart monitor and busy sounds of medical staff scurrying about outside of her room gave away her location. She was in a hospital, but she had no idea how she had gotten there. *He told me to leave town. If he gets wind that I survived and that I'm here, he'll come finish the job.*

Panicked, her body temperature began to rise and her pulse raced as fear caused her adrenaline to soar. Mecca had instilled a permanent terror in her heart. She had never been afraid of anyone, until now. Not even God had taught her a lesson so tough. Mecca had given her the craving to live, and in order to do that she had to get out of Miami . . . fast.

Her panic caused the machines around her to sound off and she cursed herself silently. Miamor knew that the police would undoubtedly have questions for her that she wasn't prepared to answer.

She closed her eyes just as the handle on the door twisted open. Playing possum, she listened to the commotion around her.

"What's going on with our Jane Doe?" the doctor asked.

"Blood pressure is up, heart rate is elevated," a nurse responded. Miamor lay still as they checked her vitals. With her eyes closed and ears open she listened carefully.

"She is lucky that those kids found her when they did. Another day and she might not have made it," the nurse said with sympathy in her voice. "I can't imagine why someone would hurt a young woman this way. With her injuries, I'm surprised she is even alive."

The doctor, focused on his job, merely grunted a reply. He had seen much worse in his ten years on the job. He wasn't emotionally attached to the patients like the young, novice nurse. "Monitor her closely," he finally said as he jotted notes on Miamor's chart. "As soon as she wakes up, inform me and call this detective." The doctor handed the nurse a card. "He would like to speak with her immediately. They're running her prints now to see if they can gather some information on her."

Miamor's internal alarm sounded off. She was in trouble. If those fingerprints came back, her juvenile records would pop up, giving them her government name. She had committed so many murders over the years that there was no telling how many times she had slipped up. In her mind, she had been so careful, so untouchable when she hit her marks, but all it took was one mistake . . . one partial fingerprint to lead the police directly to her. Every doorknob she had ever touched was now threatening her anonymity. Had she been careful, every time, all the time? Miamor couldn't be so sure. Miamor tortured herself as she scrolled through her mental Rolodex, recalling every nigga she had ever hit, but the possibilities were endless. If those fingerprints came back, her freedom was in jeopardy.

She waited until the nurse and doctor left the room before she shot up out of her bed. I've got to get out of here, now!

She reached over and shut off the machines, then ripped the IV out of the front of her hand, wincing as blood tricked down her wrist.

"Hmm!" she grunted while using all of her might to meander out of the bed and stand to her feet. They instantly gave out underneath her, and she fell hard to the cold tile floor. Miamor gripped the side of the bed, struggling to pull herself to her feet as she kept her eyes trained on the door. What should have been an easy task took all of her effort as perspiration gathered on her forehead. She steadied herself, panting hard as she willed her knees not to buckle. Her legs trembled like leaves in the wind and threatened to give out at any moment. Miamor had never been so weak in her life. The painkillers they had filled her with numbed the pain, but did nothing to erase her fatigue.

Miamor's fear was greater than anything she had ever felt. Her back was against a wall, and Mecca had taken all of the fight out of her. She struggled over to the door, using the bedrails as support as she slowly made her way across the room. Her body urged her to quit, but desperation fueled her shaky limbs.

By the time she made it to the door, she felt as if she had run a marathon. The thin fabric of the hospital gown clung to her sweaty body, and her eyes were wide in alert. Nothing had ever taken so much energy or effort to accomplish.

The walls of the hospital were the equivalent to death row. She was just waiting around to die . . . waiting for Mecca to get wind of her whereabouts and come finish the job as he had promised. The light in the hallway blinded her as she put her bare feet on the cold tile. Miamor felt the room spin, and she closed her eyes as she leaned against the wall to keep herself upright. Her deep breaths calmed the world around her, and when she opened her eyes a few stray tears slid down her cheeks.

*Overwhelmed, she took a step, avoiding eye contact
with everyone around her as she crept along the wall.
Nurses and doctors hurriedly bypassed her, too busy to
notice that she was out of place. Miamor slid into the
first supply closet she found. She rummaged through
it silently, taking everything she could possibly need.
When she found a pair of nurses' scrubs folded on the
shelf, she immediately changed into them, knowing
that they would help her blend in with the other workers.*

*Miamor tossed the hospital gown and stuffed gauze,
alcohol pads, and a scalpel into her pockets before
exiting again. This time, no one noticed her and she fit
right in as she made her way slowly to the elevators
on her floor. If anyone had looked down, her shoeless
feet would have given her away.*

*She slid into the elevators and sighed in relief as
they shut behind her. Miamor's body was threatening to
shut down, but she knew that if she lost her strength,
she was dead.*

DING.

*The elevator doors opened in the lobby and when
Miamor saw the entrance to the hospital, her heart
fluttered. She was so close to freedom that she could
taste it. Miamor walked out into the lobby, but when
she saw three uniformed police officers enter the
building, she halted. She turned instantly and crept
into the stairwell, heading down.*

*"Fuck! Fuck! Fuck!" she whispered as she half ran,
half stumbled down the flight of steps. She burst into
the basement, but stopped in shock when she saw the
dead bodies lying on cold metal slabs. Footsteps behind
her resounded as she heard someone descending the
steps. There was nowhere to run. Like a fly trapped in*

a spider's web, Miamor was stuck, and in her current state she was too weak to fight.

Miamor rushed over to the wall and fear pulsed through her. The steel wall housed metal drawers where bodies could be stored. Miamor pulled open a drawer, finding a stiff, cold body lying on a slab. She quickly closed it and moved to the next drawer. Another body. She looked back at the door, hearing a man's voice as it drew near. She rushed to the next drawer. She breathed a sigh of relief when she saw that it was empty. She climbed on top of the metal slab and shuddered when she thought of how many lifeless souls had lain there before her. Her stomach turned and she felt as if she would throw up. Doing the unthinkable, she slid the drawer closed.

The instant drop in temperature caused her to shiver. Her chest heaved as if she had just run a marathon, and her mind played tricks on her as she imagined the bodies around her. It was so cold that her teeth chattered, and she covered her mouth, blowing into her hands to create some warmth.

The space that she was in was so tight that she could barely move. Claustrophobia set in as Miamor began to feel trapped. She had always been so composed, so strategic, but at this moment she was feeling emotional, irrational, and the death that surrounded her sent chills down her spine. Miamor wasn't used to being so vulnerable, and if she didn't get out of there she would crack.

She listened as the coroner worked, listening to music and humming carefree while she froze inside her hiding spot. She didn't know how long she would make it without giving herself away. Suddenly the entire refrigerator illuminated and Miamor gasped as one of the metal slabs slid out. Miamor looked left, then right, and her eyes widened in horror as she realized how many dead bodies surrounded her. Some of them hadn't even been processed yet. Open gunshot wounds and lifeless eyes were all around. Her hands trembled as she cupped her mouth and she quickly snapped her eyes closed. It felt like she was lying in her own coffin, and if she didn't calm herself she would explode. Her anxiety built as tears of frustration overwhelmed her.

Stay quiet . . . just stay quiet, she urged herself.

The clang of the drawer closing caused her heart to drop into her stomach. This had to be punishment for the murder count she had racked up. Now death was outnumbering her, and she felt as if she was going to lose it.

Miamor was tortured for four hours as she waited for the coroner's shift to end. When she finally heard the coroner leave for the night, her limbs were so frozen that her body was numb. Miamor pushed her feet against the wall in front of her, causing the drawer to burst open. Her blue lips trembled and her teeth chattered as she climbed down.

Miamor stumbled toward the counter and leaned against it for support as she shivered uncontrollably. Her entire body tensed when she heard the door to the morgue clatter open. Like a deer in headlights she turned around. A middle-aged woman in a white lab coat stared back at her, stunned.

"Hey! What are you doing down here? This area is—"

Miamor doubled over and groaned in pain, clenching her abdomen, interrupting the woman's line of questioning.

"Oh goodness! Are you okay?" the woman asked as she crossed the room to come to Miamor's aid. It was the biggest mistake she could have made. Miamor slid the ten-inch scalpel from the pocket of her stolen scrubs and using all of her strength, she arose and wrapped her arm around the woman's neck.

"If you move or scream, I'll slit your throat from ear to ear. You got me?" she asked.

The woman was scared shitless and nodded her head in compliance.

"Now, who else are you expecting to come down here?" Miamor asked. The woman was paralyzed in horror, and Miamor pricked her skin with the blade, causing a small trail of blood to begin to flow.

"Please don't hurt me," the woman pleaded.

"Then answer my question," Miamor said. She was so weak that the woman could have easily overpowered her, but she kept her voice steady, deadly, and strong, hoping that the woman didn't test her.

"No one. I'm the third shift coroner. I work alone," she replied. "Are you going to kill me?"

"If you do what I say, you'll be fine," Miamor said truthfully.

Miamor's mind spun as Mecca's threats clouded her judgment. He'd told her to disappear. Miamor knew that she had no choice but to run—run and never look back. The only problem was the two bad bitches she was leaving behind. Aries and Robyn would never stop looking for her. As long as they thought she was alive, then their loyalty would keep them searching for her. I've got to die, she thought.

"Sit on your hands in the corner," she ordered. The woman did as she was told as Miamor walked over to the wall of the dead. She began pulling out the drawers, one by one, until she came across one that suited

her—a black girl who was too young to be lying life-less before her. The tag on her toe read JANE DOE.

Damn, Miamor thought.

"I need her hands," Miamor choked out. Not even she believed what she was about to do. Mecca was pushing her to the brink of insanity. Her fear and desperation forced her to take drastic measures.

"What?" the woman responded.

"I need you to cut off her fucking hands," Miamor snapped, this time more stern.

The woman rose to her feet and meandered toward the surgical saw. She just wanted to leave the situation alive. Avoiding eye contact with Miamor she did as she was instructed, shaking the entire time. After she was done, she put them in a plastic zip bag and handed them to Miamor.

"Please, I've done what you've asked. I have a family . . ."

Miamor walked over to grab the woman's leather briefcase. She emptied its contents onto the floor until she found the woman's wallet and keys. She grabbed her driver's license and read the woman's address aloud.

"Fifty-four seventy-one Brookgate Court, Miami, Florida."

The woman's eyes bulged.

"You have no idea who I am or what I look like. You were too fearful to look me in the face. You don't know anything. You can't remember anything. Those are the answers to your questions when the police ask. You understand?" she asked.

The woman nodded.

Miamor pulled out an empty drawer.

"Get in," she said.

The woman's eyes widened, horrified as she began to cry. But she didn't protest as she climbed on top of the slab. Miamor removed the woman's shoes and then closed the drawer.

Miamor fell backward, letting her back rest against the wall as she breathed erratically and closed her eyes. Yes, she was a killer, but she was on some other shit at the moment. Not even she had the stomach for what she was doing. She grabbed the woman's bag and stuffed the hands inside, then stuffed her feet into the coroner's shoes.

She knew she couldn't rest. She had to keep it moving. By now, the entire hospital knew that she was missing. Surely they would be looking for her. Miamor urged her legs to work as she stumbled from counter to counter, knocking over instruments and paperwork as she crossed the room. Finally she made it to the door and slowly ascended the steps. When she finally made it to the top, she was winded and sweating profusely, the scrubs clinging to her wet body. Nothing had ever been so hard to accomplish in her life, and her injuries screamed for her to stop, but she was like a shark. The minute she stopped moving she would die. The EXIT sign that hung above the door was so close yet torturously still so far away.

Everything in her wanted to call for help, needed Young Carter to use his position and power to get her out of this mess, but she couldn't. Calling him would be signing her own death certificate, because with Carter came Mecca. The blood bond they shared made her obsolete.

Miamor half walked, half stumbled as she headed to the door. Her head was down, but her eyes stayed up, scanning the room. No one noticed her as she slipped through the double doors and out into the dark night.

As soon as her feet hit concrete she ran, falling repeatedly because she was barely able to stand up.

Miamor willed herself to run faster, but the more steps she took the more hopeless her escape became. She hit the ground, her feet unable to withstand much more. She scooted her back against a parked car and gripped the scalpel in her pocket. She fished inside the bag until she located the woman's keys then hit the alarm button.

HONK! HONK! HONK!

Flashing lights and a loud car horn sounded off as Miamor looked around until she located the car. A brand-new silver CLK called her name as she brought herself to her feet and rushed to the car. Miamor started the ignition and pulled off into the night as tears finally ran down her face. She sobbed so hard that she could barely see while making her escape.

✳✳✳

Miamor stumbled inside of her apartment and quickly rushed to her safe. She pulled out the money that she had saved up. $250,000 to be exact. She then removed two 9 mm pistols. She stuffed the cash and one of the weapons into a duffel bag, putting the other gun into one of her handbags for easy access. Miamor showered quickly and threw on more comfortable clothes before grabbing her bag and kissing her life good-bye.

Miamor wiped down the stolen car, then got into her own as she put her new life together in her head. She checked into a seedy motel and gave into the pain and exhaustion that crippled her.

Miamor jumped out of her sleep and grabbed the gun from underneath her pillow all in one action, pointing it straight ahead of her. She breathed heav-

ily as she looked around, paranoid as the drapes blew from the small breeze that came through the open window. "I have to get out of here," she said. The sleep had done nothing to heal her ailing body, but it had given her enough time to clear her mind. She grabbed her car keys and headed out to her last stop.

✳✳✳

The sound of bells opening announced her presence as Miamor entered the tattoo shop. Tattoo art drawings covered the walls, and she looked around impressed, knowing that she had found the perfect man for the job. The hum of the tattoo gun resounded loudly in the shop as Miamor made her way toward the back.

"Hello!" she called out.

The buzz of the tattoo gun ceased and a white boy with spiked hair and a fully art-covered torso appeared out of the back.

"What can I do for you?" he asked.

"How much for a tattoo?" she inquired.

"Depends on what you get. You got anything in mind?" he asked.

"Two words. No color. Just black. Small font," she replied.

"That'd be about seventy-five dollars," he said.

Miamor nodded to the back where she saw a young girl lying on her stomach, waiting for him to return. "If you clear the shop, I'll pay $7500," she offered.

The tattoo artist chuckled slightly and began to turn away from her. "What kinda bullshit you on, sweetheart?" he said dismissively. She pulled out a knot of money and tossed it to him, instantly piquing his interest. He thumbed through the bills, finding all

Benjamin Franklin faces staring back at him. "Give me five minutes."

Miamor smirked and waited until the shop was empty before she proceeded.

"So what you want tattooed?" he asked.

Miamor pulled out the clear bag and tossed it to him. "These."

The man jumped back, letting the hands hit the floor as he knocked all of the tattoo guns on the floor. "Holy shit!" he cursed. "Where'd you get those from? Are you insane?"

Miamor calmly sat down. "Lower your voice. Rule number one: don't ask me any questions. Rule number two: you've got an hour to get it done," she said. "Now are you in or out? Because if not, I'll be taking my $7500 to the next mu'fucka."

The man weighed his options in his head: his morality or the wad of money he gripped in his hand. As tightly as he was holding it, he knew that he wasn't passing up the opportunity. He'd have to do a hundred tattoos to make that kind of dough.

"I'll do it."

He picked up the bag with his thumb and index finger, feeling his stomach turn. "This is some freaky shit," the tattoo artist stammered as he wiped the sweat from his forehead.

"Stop bitching and just do it," Miamor stated. "I need you to emulate this perfectly. Same font and everything." Miamor held out her own wrists to show the white boy her own artwork: MURDER MAMAS

The tattoo artist went to work, copying the tattoo perfectly, and when he was done he sat back in admiration.

"Think it's a perfect match," he said.

Miamor looked and nodded in approval. The man turned to bag the hands.

BOOM!

Miamor sent a bullet through the back of his skull. She hated to do it, but he didn't seem like the type to keep quiet, and she couldn't risk anyone knowing she was alive.

She grabbed the hands and put them in the prepackaged box then dropped them at the nearest shipping store on her route out of town. The next day Aries and Robyn would receive "her hands" on the doorstep of their Los Angeles home. Once they did, there would be no one else to come looking for her. She would be dead to the world, dead to her old life, and she could heed Mecca's warning to forget that a girl named Miamor ever existed. It was time for her to start a new life.

Chapter 7

"I've never murked anybody
that didn't deserve it."
—Miamor

Miamor jumped out of her sleep, panting and gasping for air. She covered her racing heart with her hand and closed her eyes until her pulse slowed. The nightmares of her past stopped her from moving forward. Every night she dreamt of how she had escaped Mecca's clutches, but it seemed as though he still had her mind imprisoned in fear. She arose from the bed and wrapped her body in the sheets as she left the room in search of Carter. Miamor was being given a second chance at life. All she had to do was let go of the past, but it was easier said than done.

The sound of a crackling fire drew her toward Carter's study. She stepped inside and was immediately taken aback by the beautiful room. His home was so massive that she had not yet explored it all. In fact, their reunion had been contained to the bedroom. They couldn't get enough of one another, and this was the first time she had taken notice of her new surroundings. The walls consisted of bookshelves that went from the floor to the top of the twenty-five-foot ceilings, the lighting was low, and the mahogany furniture was antique. A king's throne sat behind his desk, and it was so fitting because Carter truly was royalty. A leather sofa sat off to the right, directly in front of the glowing fire that Carter stared right into.

"It's late. What are you doing up?" he asked. His back was toward her and he never looked her way, but he felt her presence as soon as she entered the room.

"I can't sleep," Miamor replied as she shifted uncomfortably. She didn't know if she should sit or stand, stay or leave. Things between her and Carter were still quite tense. They were getting reacquainted all over again, and this time she held no secrets. He knew all of her, and she was sure that there were parts of her that he didn't approve of.

"Join the club, ma," Carter stated. "I haven't gotten a wink since you came back. It's hard to rest around someone like you." Carter never fully let his guard down around Miamor. The trust in their relationship was fragile and in need of repair. He knew that rebuilding their foundation would take time.

His words knocked the wind out of her as she realized that he thought the worst of her. "I would never hurt you, Carter. I've never murked anybody that didn't deserve it. I'm not a monster, and the niggas I've come at always saw it coming," she said, slightly offended. "Maybe I shouldn't have come here," she said, speaking more to herself than at him.

She shook her head, feeling foolish for ever believing that he could accept her past.

"Miamor." Carter's voice echoed against the walls and halted her steps. "Come over here, ma."

Her feet moved obediently. This man was the only person on earth who could make her do anything. It was as if he had her under a spell. She wanted to follow his lead. Wherever he may take her, she wanted to be the woman behind him. She would obey any rule just to keep him. A born leader, Miamor had always been hard to tame, but with Carter she found herself wanting to submit. She needed him to have faith in her—faith that she could change.

She walked over to the couch that he sat on and kneeled in front of him as she raised her eyes to match his intense gaze.

Carter cupped her face in his hands. "I apologize, ma. I want you here. There's just a lot going on right now. My brother Monroe is back," Carter said.

Miamor's eyes widened in shock. She had seen Monroe's body lying cold and stiff in a casket years ago. "From the dead?" she gasped.

Carter smirked and let out a chuckle. "Seems that way, yes. It's a long story, but now that he's returned things will be complicated. I have a lot on my mind, but I don't mean to take it out on you."

"And what about us? Your family will never accept me. They won't forgive me for the things I've done," Miamor said.

"The only person's acceptance that you need to worry about is mine. Nobody else matters. No harm will come your way, no old scores will be settled. You get a pass because of me. Niggas ain't got to like it, but they will respect it. For now no one even needs to know that you're here. I have to think of a way to introduce you back into their lives without causing more conflict. Until then I need you to lay low, be unseen. You think you can handle that?"

Miamor nodded her head and replied, "Yes." Everything about Carter was intoxicating to Miamor. The way that he stuck up for her warmed her heart. She stood to her feet and dropped the sheet that covered her naked body. The amber hue from the fireplace provided the only light in the room and outlined the silhouette of her body.

His hands found her hips and he pulled her closer to him. His mouth was perfectly aligned with her womanhood, and he didn't hesitate to explore it. His warm, thick tongue opened her southern lips as he licked her gently. Circling her clit while French kissing her lips, he feasted on Miamor's sweet honey pot.

"Ohh," she moaned as she massaged the back of his head while falling victim to his head game. Her legs weakened as Carter took her love button between his teeth. Gently he bit down and Miamor lost her mind. "What are you doing to me?" she asked as began to quiver in ecstasy. Carter inserted one finger, then two, then three inside of her. Miamor's body was so responsive to his touch that she rode his hand, squeezing her vaginal muscles around his fingers as he tickled her insides and palmed her clit. Carter curved his fingers, hitting her G-spot.

"Wait. Ooh no, wait, Carter," she whispered. The pressure was building inside of her and she felt as if she would pee on herself. It felt so good that she didn't want to stop it. Her pussy lips were so swollen that it looked as if he had beat it up, and her clit throbbed for attention.

"Put your mouth on me, baby," she whispered. Carter's fingers worked her over as he simultaneously kissed her clit, and that was all she wrote. Miamor screamed as her love came down. Warmth came over her as her head fell back in sheer bliss.

Carter licked her gently as he looked up at her with sincere eyes. He was hypnotizing her with his slow rhythm, and she felt obliged to return the favor. She pushed his forehead back, depriving herself of his vicious head game, and he sat back on the leather couch. At lightning speed she had his manhood in her hands, stroking his length and tracing the veins that throbbed in his shaft.

Carter's dick was perfectly thick and long, but most importantly he knew how to use it. He pulled her down onto his lap and filled her walls. Miamor worked her hips and relaxed her muscles, allowing him total access to her body.

His body was so tense and she rode him into relaxation. She felt the stress leaving him with every move she put on him. His fingers dug into her hips as he lifted then lowered her onto his girth. Their rhythm was slow, sensual, and he pulled her taut nipple into his mouth. Bolts of electric pleasure shot up her spine, and Miamor picked up her pace, grinding into him with passion.

He palmed her voluptuous behind, spreading her cheeks in an effort to go deeper. He flipped her over, wanting to take control as he rocked into her. Carter was knocking the bottom out of her pussy, pushing her to the threshold between pleasure and pain. He slow- stroked her, exploring parts of her body that she didn't even know existed.

Her nails staked her claim as she clawed at his back. She opened her eyes as she took in all of him. Every muscle in his toned physique flexed as he handled her body. His brown complexion glistened in sweat as his face contorted in pleasure. Carter Jones was a work of art. The man was a masterpiece. He kissed her lips, and the feeling of his tongue dancing in her mouth, the taste of her sweet mouth took him over the edge. His lovemaking quickened and he went deeper, and deeper, and deeper.

"Ohh shit, ma," he bellowed, his voice a masculine grunt.

"Cum inside me, Carter," she whispered as tears came to her eyes.

He stopped briefly, panting, as he looked in her eyes.

She nodded her head. "Put a baby in me, Carter," she confirmed. Carter placed his forehead against hers and looked her in the eyes as he pumped inside of her until he spilled his seed inside of her womb.

"I love you, ma," Carter said. "I don't want to, but I do. A lesser man would never admit that to you, but I don't want there to be any indiscretions between us. Our home has to be strong. I have too much to lose to allow anarchy into my world."

"I will love you until our end, Carter," Miamor replied before falling asleep in his arms.

Chapter 8

"We just trying to get money
and stay off the radar."
—Young Carter

Money definitely was not going to waste any time.
He wanted to get acclimated to the new regime
quickly. Monroe longed to take over the streets of
Miami once again. He wanted to take back the throne
and then retire at the top like his father was supposed
to do. Also, to cope with his losses he would have to
stay busy. He wanted to get into the swing of things
and build the empire that had fallen during his extended slumber. Therefore, Carter set up a meeting
with the head soldiers of their crew, along with Zyir,
to meet and reintroduce Monroe to the streets and the
"new look" Cartel.

The rendezvous was at an empty warehouse that Zyir
had been leasing. It was where they kept the coke and
guns hidden. The steel doors and concrete floors gave
the place a cold feel. Steel gates separated portions of
the facility, and the only sound was the loud buzzing
from the light. A single card table sat square in the
middle of the floor, with a single beam of light shining
directly down on it.

The mechanical door rose and in came Carter's black
Range Rover, followed by a black tinted SUV driven
by Zyir. Zyir had his soldiers with him, and they were

about six deep. All of them were under twenty-one, but all of them were also live wires and would do anything at Zyir's command. They were all excited and also nervous about meeting the notorious Monroe "Money" Diamond. They all grew up admiring him and when he "died" it only made his legacy grow. While Mecca had the streets in fear when he was alive, Monroe had the love. He had swagger, a gentle kindness, and the muscle that made for a great gangster. But those days were gone, and they would soon find out that Monroe wasn't the same as he once was.

Everyone got out of the cars and gathered around the table, waiting for Money to arrive. Zyir and Carter slapped hands, and Carter nodded at the young soldiers as they formed a circle.

"Where is ya man?" Zyir asked as he checked his watch, referring to Money.

"I told him ten. He should be pulling up any minute now," Carter said as he glanced at his wrist and checked his watch.

"Well, he's late," Zyir said, not really liking the idea of adding someone to their crew. However, out of respect for Young Carter he would not raise any sand.

"I've been here. I'm never late, homeboy," Money said as he stepped out of the shadows, startling all of them. They all reached for their guns and froze when they realized it was Money. He walked over to the table and joined the men. He and Carter embraced, and Monroe looked around the table and was disgusted. Back in his day, young niggas couldn't even be in his presence. They hadn't lived enough or experienced enough in life to be at a table with a boss in his eyes, so he immediately was turned off by the situation. His body language told it all as he mugged each of the youngsters as Carter began to talk.

"I want to introduce you to the crew. This is Bo, Fly Boogie, and Damon. And of course you know Zyir. This is who holds everything down," Carter stated. Fly Boogie, a skinny kid with a knack for fashion, was the first to speak.

"Yo, it's a pleasure to meet you, big homie. You're like a legend in Miami," he said as he extended his open hand to greet Money. Money looked down at Fly Boogie's hand with a blank expression on his face. He then looked at Carter in disbelief and chuckled.

"Let's get this meeting started," Money said as he totally ignored Fly Boogie as if he wasn't even there.

Zyir looked at Carter and shook his head discreetly. Zyir didn't like the fact that Money dismissed his man, but he opted to stay quiet.

"Okay, this is how it is. We have a sweet connect in Brazil on the coke. He goes by the name of Buttons. We get it catered to us for an extra twenty percent. He brings it over to the port of Miami and we get it fresh off of the boat. We run through about one hundred joints a month," Carter said as he began to slowly walk around the table as he explained the workings of their business.

"I take care of the distribution, and once it gets off the boat, I take it straight to the streets. We have about twenty trap houses around the city, and we work out of them. We have friends down at the police department to keep us in the know on any investigations or random raids. It's pretty simple," Zyir explained as he rubbed his hands together while helping Carter explain.

"That's right. It is very simple. I was thinking you can play the back and let Zyir handle the day to day since we got a smooth operation going on. Maybe try to look for some sources to clean up the money so we can transition, feel me?" Carter said, now looking directly at Money.

"Play the back?" Monroe repeated as he looked at Carter as if he was crazy. He didn't like the sound of Carter's plan. He was ready to jump headfirst into the game and take over all that was lost. The "new" Cartel couldn't hold a candle to what Monroe had left behind. "You only have twenty houses in all of Miami? When did we downgrade to running trap houses, huh? My father started this thing of ours, and it wasn't meant to move fifty bricks a month. We did that in a day!"

"Calm down, homie. We—" Zyir said, trying to ease the building tension that was forming.

"And who the fuck are you?" Monroe asked, interrupting Zyir. He wasn't trying to talk to anyone except his brother. He was tired of beating around the bush. He was the boss and he wanted to make it known.

Immediately Zyir's goons put their hands on their waists, ready to bust. At that point they didn't care who Monroe was. He was disrespecting their boss and they were ready to get busy. All of their eyes were on Zyir, and if Zyir would have given the slightest indication for them to react, Money would have been Swiss cheese.

"Just give me the green light," Fly Boogie whispered to Zyir without moving his lips. Money smirked at Fly Boogie's comment and slid his hand to his waist where his gun rested.

"Everyone calm down!" Carter demanded as Zyir and Money stared at each other tensely, both of them clenching their jaws tightly. Carter continued, "Money, you have been gone a long time. I'm not trying to box you out. I just want you to ease into this. It's not how it was five years ago. Feds are on us, and with all the murders from the last war, it made us hot. We just trying to stay low, get money, and stay off the radar. It's a new day, bruh."

"You sound crazy right now. Instead of having ten cops on payroll, you should pay the chief of police. Everybody has a price! That means you only have to deal with one person rather than ten. Also, why aren't we wholesaling? Who runs trap houses? *We move weight!* Back in my day, little niggas like this couldn't even be in my presence. But now, you bringing them to the table?" Monroe ranted, pointing out every flaw he saw in Carter's system.

Carter, wanting to be diplomatic, kept his cool and knew that he had to take control before it got out of hand. "I need everyone to leave now. Money, let's talk," Carter said as he stepped to the side, giving Zyir and his crew a clear path to the truck they pulled up in. No one moved until Zyir nodded his head and then just like that, they headed to their cars. Zyir followed close behind and stopped just as he walked past Carter.

"You good?" Zyir asked, not knowing whether he should leave Carter alone with Money.

"Yeah, I'm good. I'll call you later," Carter confirmed and put one hand on Zyir's shoulder. Zyir shot a look at Money, and they exchanged menacing stares as he walked away. Carter tapped Monroe on the chest to try to break the tension between the two of them. "Let's talk."

"Seem like there is nothing to talk about. You have everything figured out I see," Monroe said sarcastically and released a small smirk. Carter shook his head at Monroe's answer and put his hands together as he thought about Monroe's viewpoint.

"Listen, I know what it seemed like, but it's the way it's going to be. Just give it a couple of weeks and feel everything out before you jump in," Carter said, trying to be as diplomatic as possible.

"Feel things out? I was moving weight when you were back in Michigan small timing. Remember that, my nigga! But you know what; I'm going to play the back. You right," Monroe said, easing off of his hostility. He knew at that moment that it was a line drawn in the sand, and he understood what side he stood on. He kicked himself for expressing his frustrations and knew that the old him would have never let anyone know what he was thinking. *I am a little rusty I see,* he thought as he looked at Carter, trying to read his mind.

Carter clenched his jaws at Monroe's remark, but didn't show any emotion. If that had been anyone else, Carter would have rocked him to sleep just off of GP. Nevertheless, the calculating boss just released a small smile and put his hand on Monroe's shoulder. "Listen, I meet the connect in a couple days. To show you that I'm not trying to box you out . . . I want to introduce you to him," Carter suggested.

"That's what I'm talking about. Let's get to the money," Money said calmly as he rubbed both of his hands together.

Carter noticed something strange about Monroe. His mannerisms weren't like he remembered. Everything about Monroe reminded Carter of Mecca. Carter chalked it up to guilt playing with his own mind, but he knew Monroe wasn't quite the same as he remembered. It was as if Mecca's soul had flown into Monroe.

Carter quickly shook off the notion and began to break down the logistics to his brother and caught him up on what was going on in the streets. In addition to breaking down the product and flooding the streets, they were heavy in wholesale. The Cartel was getting all the money from the bottom up, and he hoped that Monroe could see that they had a good thing going. However, in the back of his mind Carter knew it could all go bad if Monroe ever found out that he killed Mecca. Only time would tell how it would unravel, but until then . . .

***

The private jet landed on the airstrip in Brazil. Inside were the pilot, Carter, Monroe, and Zyir. They were landing there to meet their coke connect, Buttons, a tall, fair-skinned Brazilian who specialized in the coke business. Carter had met him a year back while being there for Breeze's wedding.

As the plane doors lifted up Monroe's heart began to rapidly beat. It was something that only a hustler could relate to. The rush and allure of getting to the money was like an adrenaline rush for a street nigga, and Monroe's burning flame for the streets had been dormant for years. It had just been relit. He was ready to put his staple in the game. He was still very young and had the world ahead of him. He looked over at Zyir, who remained quiet the entire flight, and knew that he would eventually be a problem.

The Brazilian setup was beautiful. Gorgeous women with bronze skin were everywhere, and the land itself was stunning. The narrow streets and tall brick buildings had their own personality, and Monroe was amazed as he took in the sight. They all sat in the back of a Jeep that Buttons had sent for them as they maneuvered through the bumpy roads, on their way to Buttons' cocaine sanctum.

"Here it is," Carter said as they approached the massive brick warehouse. The place was surrounded by steel gates, and vicious pit bulls ran freely within them. Monroe looked at the top of the building and saw young gunmen with assault rifles and binoculars. None of the gunmen looked to be a day over eighteen, but all had menacing stares and an eagerness to prove to their boss that they were loyal and worthy to move up in the ranks.

"Buttons is a different type of nigga. Fair warning," Carter said as they approached the gate.

Two armed goons were standing at the gate. When they pulled in, the goons immediately began to look inside the car with AK-47s in their hands. Once they saw that the coast was clear, they waved the driver in. Just like that, they were granted access to the biggest drug distribution and manufacturing business in Brazil. Rio was mostly known for its beautiful women and sexual escapades, yet the black market there was just as lucrative and successful. Just as the sexual fantasies that attracted lusting men, the pure cocaine and cheap prices drove in the drug bosses.

As the Jeep made its way through the property, the men looked at the property and how well it was secured. Buttons had shooters literally everywhere on its property. Monroe instantly knew that they were dealing with a made guy.

They pulled up to the single building that was in the rear of the property. They pulled up to the steel garage door and the driver blew the horn twice. Seconds later the door rose and exposed the factory-like assembly line where the coke was being cut, measured, and packaged for distribution.

Buttons stood at the top tier that overlooked the whole operation. He stood six foot three inches and had the stature of a model. His long, curly hair was pulled back tightly into a ponytail as he slowly paced back and forth, overseeing his operation. He smoked a cigar and took his time as he deeply inhaled, letting the Cuban smoke dance on his lungs. Buttons was the kingpin of Rio and had a long history with the sale of cocaine. He had political connections and was literally untouchable inside of his country. He took a liking to Carter because of his business savvy and consistency.

Carter led the pack as they walked on to the floor and in between the long tables full of coke. Everyone seemed to be focused on their particular job and not on Carter and his crew. Buttons stopped pacing and looked down at Carter.

"Carter! Glad you could make it," he said with open arms and a smile. Buttons made his way down the stairs followed closely by a young Brazilian gunman.

"Buttons. Thanks for having us," Carter said as he walked toward Buttons and shook hands with him. Carter then turned around and looked at Zyir and Money. "Of course, you remember Zyir," Carter said. Buttons nodded his head at Zyir, acknowledging him. Carter turned to Monroe and nodded toward him. "This is my brother, Monroe."

"Monroe. How are you? I am Buttons," he said with a heavy accent.

"I'm good," Monroe said as he stepped forward and extended his hand to Buttons. Buttons shook his hand and was impressed with Monroe's demeanor and fearlessness. While Zyir usually played the back, Monroe wanted to make his presence known; Buttons sensed this.

The rendezvous was about an hour, and Carter discussed a bigger shipment with Buttons, and Monroe listened closely and analyzed their business relationship. For what Carter was getting them for, Monroe used to get them for half that price when he was over The Cartel. Monroe's mind immediately began to churn, thinking about a master plan. He saw a lot of holes in their operations and wondered why Carter was copping from a Brazilian connect who was obviously taxing him. Little did Monroe know, Estes had retired from the drug game and didn't give his connections to Young Carter. Estes didn't believe in connecting people who weren't blood. So the connects ended when Mecca died. Monroe already began to make plans to return to see Buttons, but the next time Monroe would come alone. He would be coming to sell and not to buy cocaine.

As they wrapped up the meeting with handshakes, Monroe made sure he looked Button in the eyes and said, "I'll see you soon. Very soon." Carter didn't realize it, but he had just introduced Buttons to his competition.

Hours later they were back on the jet, and Carter looked over at Monroe, who seemed to be in deep thought, staring out of the window while resting his index finger on his temple.

"I just brought you to the table. I introduced you to the connect. Hopefully you understand now that I want you to play the back only temporarily," Carter said as he poured himself a glass of cognac, Louis XIII to be exact.

"No doubt. I understand now. Let's get it," Monroe said, but his eyes didn't match his words. He was thinking about how he was about to box both of them out and take over the streets once again. "I am the son of Carter Diamond. Miami is mine," he said as he sat back comfortably and closed his eyes with a small grin.

Zyir watched closely as he remained quiet. He was growing to dislike Monroe more and more by the minute.

Needless to say, when they returned to the States, Monroe turned right back around and headed back to Rio to see Buttons. As Monroe made his way through the airport, he called his grandfather, Estes.

"Papa, I need a favor," Monroe said as soon as he heard his grandfather's voice on the opposite side of the line.

"Anything for you," Estes said in his usual low and raspy voice. It seemed as if Monroe could hear the cigar smoke in his grandfather's lungs as he spoke.

"I need you to make a couple of calls on my behalf. I need my father's old connect. I need you to make that happen pronto," Monroe said as he made his way to his boarding gate.

"Enough said. I was wondering what was taking you so long. I will set up a sit down immediately," Estes said as if it was a cake walk.

"Yeah. It is about that time. I'm not liking what I am seeing. A lot has changed since I was away."

"I agree. I never extended the family's connections because I am a firm believer in keeping the family's name reputable. I couldn't trust those that weren't my blood to uphold that. You understand?" Estes said, dropping game on his only male bloodline.

"Understood. Let's make it happen. I will be back in town in a couple days. Prices are still the same?" he asked.

"Indeed. They never change for customers like us," Estes explained as he alluded to the coke prices that his connections offered. People like Estes had connections that never raised prices, no matter how the market was. At that level of drug dealing, bosses sold for the sport . . . not for the money.

Now that Monroe had convinced Estes to introduce him to his Miami connect, it was the beginning of Monroe's second era. Monroe figured since Carter wanted him to play the backseat, he would just rather take over the whole vehicle. It was Monroe's turn to take back the streets . . . his way. He was about to make Buttons an offer he could not refuse.

Chapter 9

"Let the games begin, gentlemen."
—Monroe

Zyir rode through the city, and in a matter of weeks the streets had dried up. It looked like a ghost town. From Opa-locka to Carol City, all the way to Little Havana, all of his operations were at a standstill and nobody was getting paid.

As he pulled up to Seventieth Street and Fifth Avenue he was more than livid. His most profitable blocks were turning no profit, and this alarmed him. He parked his black S-Class along the curb and checked his surroundings. The notorious hood was known worldwide for its ruthless stick-up kids, and Zyir made sure that he was acutely aware of everything moving around him. He pressed a button on his custom radio console, and a hidden compartment slid out. He grabbed the handgun that lay inside and tucked it in his waistline before exiting the vehicle.

He approached the small project building, and all eyes were on him. Zyir was the smallest nigga on the block, but he had the heart of a lion. Slim in stature, many men had learned the hard way by sizing him up at first glance. Zyir didn't pop his gums, he popped his guns, so anyone he had ever caught beef with usually didn't live to tell about it. He had made an example out of plenty since arriving in Miami, which was why as he approached he was shown nothing but respect. The littered streets were unusually quiet.

"What up, baby?" he greeted Fly Boogie, one of the young'uns who worked as a lookout. Fly Boogie leaned against the graffiti-tagged wall and was the perfect definition of a new school hustler. Fresh Adidas kicks laced his feet. He wore rock-washed skinny jeans that sagged slightly off his hips, and a white wife beater. His snap back hat, nerd glasses, and chain belt accessorized his outfit. At first glance he looked like a skater kid; one would never guess that he was a thorough shooter. His body count was official. He was never afraid of a gun battle, which was why he was the perfect lookout. He would peel a nigga cap back and ask questions later. No one was coming near Zyir's trap spot unless they were already authorized to be there. Fly Boogie made sure of it.

"Ain't shit up 'round here. We dry than a muuu'fucka," Fly Boogie said in his heavy Southern drawl.

Zyir frowned because that was the exact same response he had gotten from each of his spots. Shit had slowed up, and most of his lieutenants were out of product. This was unusual when each of his spots usually blew through five bricks each week, easy. "What happened to the shipment? Shit just came in yesterday? Why that work ain't ready yet?" Zyir questioned.

"Maannn, you gotta ask them niggas," Fly Boogie responded. "You know I'm just the lookout. As long as I don't see them red and blues or no niggas lurking then I'm good. I don't worry too much about that other shit, Zy. I play my position, you feel me?"

Zyir kept his hand near his hip as he hooked his fingers in his belt loop and nodded his head. "Yeah, I feel you, fam. Keep an eye on my whip. If the police roll by here, drive my shit around the block," he instructed as he pulled out a knot of money and peeled off a one hundred dollar bill for the young kid.

"No doubt," Fly Boogie responded as he shook his head and pushed Zyir's hand away. "I got you, fam. It's not necessary. I'm sitting here anyway. It's my job to patrol the block. Your car good, bro. Handle your business," he said.

Zyir liked the kid's style. Most thirsty niggas would have pocketed his money, but Fly Boogie was loyal. He felt honored for a dude of Zyir's stature to even talk to him, let alone trust him with his car.

Zyir tossed him his car key and ascended the steps that led to the second level of the raggedy apartment building. He operated out of every unit on the top floor. There were four in all. One was where the coke was cooked; in the second unit his young'uns stacked the dough; the third served as an artillery closet with every type of automatic weapon in that apartment; and the fourth was a parlay spot for his workers.

He knocked four times on the door in a distinct rhythm, and a small rectangular peephole slid to the side. He was allowed inside immediately upon recognition.

"Hey, Zy!" the ladies called out sweetly as he walked through the apartment, headed toward the back. Ten beautiful stallions stood in high heels and nothing more, cooking up hard for the fiends and bagging powder cocaine for the free base users. There was so much product cooking in the small space that Zyir could smell the distinctive scent in the air. He walked directly toward the back and entered the bedroom, which functioned as a small office.

"Zyir, what's good, baby?" Angel, his head lieutenant, greeted.

"You tell me," Zyir said. "From what I'm hearing nobody's making money. Where's the shipment? I pay you the most because I give you the most responsibility, fam. If you can't handle your position, it's a lot of hungry mu'fuckas under you who would love the opportunity to step up."

Zyir wasn't one to raise his voice, but just from his disposition Angel could tell that his boss wasn't pleased.

"I don't want to have to come all the way to your side of town only to find out that my money is short. Fuck is going on, fam?" Zyir asked.

"The shipment wasn't on deck, and we running off of last month's product. It's only a matter of time before this shit runs out. Plus niggas ain't fucking with us. Some new mu'fuckas set up shop out in Hialeah. They selling the shit for dirt cheap. Niggas is selling bricks for sixteen thousand dollars. That's them 1999 prices, you feel me? I sling these shits for that and we losing money. We can't compete with that. So anybody buying weight is going to these new niggas. We still got the lower level shit on lock, but like I said, we almost out, and if we don't re-up we gon' lose our footing in the streets real quick," Angel explained.

"I'll check on the shipment. I just met with my man, so that should have been right on time. In the meantime run the competition off the blocks. We can't compete with their prices, but they can't compete with our muscle. They can stay, but they got to pay a tax. This real estate belongs to The Cartel, so the niggas got to pay rent if they want to hustle this way. Be diplomatic, and if they buck, then we put our murder game down. I hope it doesn't come to that. In war nobody makes money," Zyir stated. He slapped hands with his man and then made his exit.

Fly Boogie threw up a salute and tossed Zyir his keys as Zyir walked by. Zyir sped off and immediately called Carter. Business with Buttons had always gone according to plan. Their dealings with him were so consistent that there was never room for error. This missed shipment was no mistake, and Zyir couldn't put his finger on it, but something fishy was in the air. He pulled out the burnout phone that he used to contact Buttons. He dialed his number from memory, knowing that the information was too sensitive to ever record.

"The number you have reached is not in service," the operator announced.

Yeah, something is most definitely up, Zyir thought. They had been doing square business with Buttons for too long for things to change now. Zyir immediately thought of their recent trip to Rio. The only factor that had changed in the situation was Monroe. He didn't know exactly what had gone down, but Zyir's hustler's intuition told him that Monroe had fucked up the game for everybody.

***

Carter sat on the wooden park bench tossing crumbs to the birds as he sat in deep contemplation. His life had come full circle, and it seemed as though all the people he had thought were lost to the game had come back to him. His family felt more complete.

Carter had handed over leadership to Zyir for good reason. The streets had sucked the life out of him. After killing Mecca, Carter knew that the game had pushed him too far and that it was time to step down. He was confident in his successor, but now that Monroe was back it created confusion. Jealousy was in the air, and Carter knew that he would have to play mediator between his blood brother and his brother by circumstance.

"Look at you, big homie, out here in the open. I know retirement don't got you slipping like that. If I wanted to get you—"

"You couldn't," Carter finished as he stood and turned around to greet Zyir, who had approached him from behind. He pointed his finger fifty yards ahead of him and then off to both sides, showing Zyir that he was never left unprotected. Three of his shooters patrolled the perimeter of the park, eyes on Carter at all times.

Carter moved like a boss. He knew the position that he had in the streets. He was like a trophy to thirsty young wolves. The reputation one could get from taking him out was enough to make him a target. The only thing that kept him secure was the respect he had earned over the years. Many niggas had the courage to take the shot, but very few had the courage to miss. Hitting Carter was easier said than done, and should someone try and fail, the repercussions were deadly.

Zyir smirked and shook his head. "I should have known," he said. The two men began to stroll through the park as Zyir filled Carter in on the situation. "I think we've got a problem with Buttons."

Carter stopped abruptly and turned toward Zyir attentively.

"The shipment didn't come in. I just left from the trap and shit is Sahara dry," Zyir stated.

"Did you call Buttons?" Carter asked.

"Line is disconnected. It's like he cut all ties with us after the meeting with Money. I know that's your bro and all, but I'm allergic to snakes, if you get my drift," Zyir said seriously. "We've been doing square business for years, and now when Money come into the picture the shit turns sour?" Zyir looked at Carter skeptically. "That sound right to you?"

Out of the corner of his eye he saw Monroe's car pull up. "Speak of the fucking devil," he mumbled as the aura turned thick.

"I've got it. Money's official. Buttons and anybody else that got a problem with him better get comfortable with his presence real quick. We've got to keep our circle strong, Zyir. All we've got is the family," Carter said seriously.

Zyir held his tongue. He had serious doubts about Monroe, but he was aware that it was a sensitive subject so he treaded lightly. Monroe approached and slapped hands with Carter.

"What it's laying like, bro?" he asked.

Carter noticed that Monroe never acknowledged Zyir. He glanced at his two brothers, one adopted through life's tests of loyalty and the other blood born. He would have to fix this divide for sure, but decided not to force it. Time would cause the two men to respect each other, or so he thought.

"I'm sending Zy back down to meet with Buttons. We out of product and suddenly he's unreachable," Carter explained.

Money nodded and smirked, knowing that he was the reason why all communication had ceased. As long as Zyir was the leader of The Cartel then the entire Cartel wouldn't eat. Monroe would make sure of it. A position of power like that had to be earned, and Zyir was handed the crown by default. Monroe would burn the entire kingdom to the ground before he allowed Zyir to rule. He definitely didn't want Carter finding out he had undermined him, however.

"You want me to fly over there and make sure everything's smooth?" he asked.

Carter shook his head. "I don't think that's wise. Zyir's more familiar with Buttons. He'll be more comfortable with him. We are easing you back into the swing of things, Money. Trust me, more responsibility will be delegated to you in due time."

Delegated to me? I'm a boss; a nigga ain't delegating shit to me. He want to send his mans to Rio, I'ma make sure he don't come back, Monroe thought angrily. He showed no signs of displeasure outwardly.

"Whatever you say. You're the boss," Monroe stated.

Carter turned to Zyir. "You'll leave in the morning."

***

Monroe sat in his car, watching as Zyir and Carter pulled off. His distaste for Zyir was growing by the day. Monroe had been away from his family for too long, and he couldn't help but feel as though he had been replaced. Monroe picked up his cell and placed a call.

"*Hola,* Monroe," Buttons answered.

"*Hola,* Buttons. I just called to give you a heads-up. Carter is sending Zyir down to Rio with his goons. He's upset that he's been cut off. They will be there tomorrow. It's in your best interest to annihilate anyone associated with The Cartel if they show up on your doorstep. They are coming to kill you. Make no mistake about it," Monroe said. He knew that if he put Buttons on the defensive, there would be no way Zyir would come back alive.

"I will prepare for their arrival," Buttons said, his voice menacingly cold.

Monroe ended the call and then checked his rearview before pulling away from the park. "Let the games begin, gentlemen."

***

Carter entered his home and for the first time since he purchased the place it felt lived in. His world had been so cold and lonely that he never appreciated the things that he had attained. The aroma of food filled the air and reminded him that he had neglected to eat. He walked into the kitchen and found Miamor over the stove. He smiled when he saw that she wore nothing but a bra and thong. Her long, shapely legs, juicy behind, and slim waist instantly sent sparks to his loins. The stilettos that graced her French-manicured feet caused him to smile. He stood back and watched her work. She clearly knew her way around a kitchen. He had missed her in his life, and her return made his entire existence complete. He walked up behind her and wrapped his arms around her waist, burying his head in the creases of her shoulder as he inhaled deeply, loving her scent.

"I could have gotten you. You didn't even know I was behind you," Carter whispered as he kissed her neck. Miamor's head fell to the side as she enjoyed the feel of his lips against her skin.

"Hmm. That feels good," she whispered. She turned toward him and kissed his lips, deeply and sensuously. "A nigga will never catch me slipping, Carter Jones. Take a look under that kitchen towel." Miamor slipped out of his embrace and walked over to the cabinet, grabbing two wine glasses.

Carter lifted the towel and saw a small-caliber pistol lying underneath it. He chuckled and thought, *Damn*.

He found her incredibly sexy. The fact that she was so thorough impressed him. He was getting to know this new side of her, and now that there were no secrets between them, he respected it. She was feminine and incredibly sexy, but the little bit of street she had in her drove him wild. She made up the perfect recipe of a woman.

"Now come have a seat and let me feed my man," she said.

"What's for dinner?" he asked as he sat down in the chair that she had pulled out for him. She was treating him like a king.

"Steak and seafood," she replied.

"And for dessert?" he quipped.

"Me," she answered.

Miamor straddled Carter. The only thing that stopped her wet pussy from soaking the crotch of his pants was the tiny fabric of her thong. The sexual chemistry that was between them was supercharged. That was the one part of their relationship that they had always gotten right.

"Or we can have dessert first," she whispered. Carter stood, lifting her as he swept everything off of the table. Dishes and silverware went flying to the floor as he laid her down on top of the expensive marble.

He removed his manhood, and in one Casanova movement he slid her thong to the side. Her wetness warmed him as he slipped inside of her. With one arm wrapped around her arched waist and the other braced against the table he controlled the pace. He stroked her slowly, powerfully, as their bodies move rhythmically.

"I love you," Miamor whispered as he kissed her neck.

His dick penetrated depths of her that she didn't even know existed. Carter's sex game was official. An unselfish lover, he always pleased her first. His touch was gentle, but he moved with authority, making commands of her without ever speaking any words.

His girth made her blossom bloom, and with every dip of his hips she matched his intensity. She grinded upward, throwing her love at him as their bodies became one. Miamor knew that she had the best pussy around. Very few had sampled it, but the ones who had were easily put under her spell. Miamor had that "make a nigga fall in love" pussy. It was inevitable to become trapped in her world, but with Carter Jones she fell just as hard. Like a magnet, she was drawn to him and not Mecca, not life, not death, could pull them apart. It was serendipitous for them to spend eternity loving each other.

Miamor closed her eyes and enjoyed the ride as she felt her orgasm build. She saw blinding white as she came, and the pulsating tool inside her along with the look of fulfillment on Carter's face told her that he had gotten his too.

He pulled out of her and grabbed her hand. "Join me in the shower, ma. I've had a long day. I just want to be around you."

"What about the food?" she asked.

"I'll have the staff wrap everything up. We'll order a pizza or something," Carter said.

It was his simplicity that endeared him to her. He could take her around the world and back. His money was long and his reach wide, but he didn't stunt to impress her. Time with her was enough to make him happy. Whether in a cardboard box or within the massive walls of his five-star mansion, they were satisfied with just the presence of one another.

Miamor followed him to the master bedroom and sat on the edge of the travertine-tiled bathtub as Carter ran the water. Vanilla bubbles and bath salts scented the room, and she lowered herself into the warm water.

Carter pulled her close, her back against his chest as they both relaxed.

"I appreciate you cooking for me. In fact, I love that, but right now no one knows you're here. You have to stay low. My family doesn't know that you've returned, and until I figure out how to handle things you have to stay inside. No more grocery runs," Carter said.

"You're right. It won't happen again," she answered. It wasn't what she wanted to say, but she was learning to bite her tongue. She was afraid that if she made one little mistake or displeased Carter in any way, he would dispel her from his life. He knew her well, however, and could tell that she wanted to say more.

"Why do you do that? You didn't used to hold anything back from me," he said.

"I'm just trying to be what you want, Carter," Miamor said. In that moment she felt small, like she was dimming her light in order to help Carter shine, something she thought she would never do for any man.

"I want a woman that speaks her mind, Miamor. Don't tiptoe around me. Respect me, be honest with me, and I will respect you and be honest with you. That's all I want from you. Now what's on your mind?" he said.

"How long do you expect for me to hide? I don't want to feel like a prisoner here," Miamor replied honestly.

"Just give me a little bit of time. I'm dealing with a lot right now," Carter admitted.

She turned around so that she could face him. His face was etched with stress.

"What's wrong?" she asked.

"Monroe and Zyir aren't on the best of terms. They aren't feeling each other. It's hard to choose one brother over another. I've got Zyir meeting with our connect tomorrow, but by selecting him to go I can tell Monroe feels slighted."

"Why don't you just make the trip yourself? That way you're not choosing sides," Miamor suggested.

Carter didn't respond, but he definitely heard what she said. It seemed to be the most diplomatic solution to his problem.

He rose from the water.

"Hey, where are you going?" she asked. "I thought we would go for round two."

Carter leaned over and kissed her lips. "Not tonight. I've got to pack and so do you. Since I can't guarantee that you'll stay put while I'm gone, you'll have to come with me. Tomorrow we're flying to Rio."

Chapter 10

"When in Rome."

—Miamor

The ocean waves washed ashore as Miamor walked through the soft white sand, leaving indents of her feet as she went. She couldn't believe that the beach was so empty. The entire coastline was clear; there wasn't a person in sight. It felt like she had the entire ocean to herself. She lifted her head to the sky and closed her eyes as the sun kissed her cheeks. Rio de Janeiro was a beautiful place, and she hoped that they found time to explore the city. She understood that they were in town so that Carter could handle his business, but certainly they could find time to play before they left. Rio was the sexiest city in the world, and Miamor wanted to fuck her man on the beach, under the stars.

She looked back and saw Carter motioning for her from the second-story balcony. She turned around and headed back to the luxury villa. She entered and found him standing in white linen shorts, a white linen shirt, and a crisp wife beater underneath. He was dapper, and Miamor smiled at how lucky she was. Carter could have any woman in the world. He could certainly have any of the sexy vixens in Rio, but he wanted her.

"I plan to meet Buttons in the morning," Carter said.

"Why not tonight?" she asked.

"Because tonight is ours," he replied. "There's no way you would ever let me live it down if I flew you in and out of Rio without letting you explore your way around."

She laughed and kissed his lips because she loved that he knew her so well.

"Well, we're in Rio and tonight I want to dance," she exclaimed.

"I don't dance, ma." Carter chuckled. "And since when do you dance, gangster?" he asked mockingly, never figuring Miamor to be the type to indulge in Latin dance.

"When in Rome, right?" she asked with a laugh.

✳✳✳

Carter and Miamor rode through the city streets presidential style as their driver escorted them to the hottest nightclub in Rio. The streets were definitely alive as the attractive people came out to play. They could see the line to the club from a block away as it looped around the building. The club was more like a hole in the wall, but it was the place to be on a Saturday night. Carter looked out the window and frowned. "You sure this is the place?" he asked the driver.

"Sí, sí," the driver replied.

"It looks like a fucking dive," he said.

"Lighten up, Carter Jones. Tonight we welcome the unexpected," she whispered.

Carter put his pistol in his waist and Miamor put a small .22 in her clutch before exiting the car. They walked straight up to the entrance, and Carter tipped the bouncer generously to be let directly into the club.

As soon as they stepped inside, Carter realized why it was so popular. The vibe was sensual, seductive, and the dance floor was packed full of people dancing to

Latin music. The club glowed red, casting an illuminating hue all over the room. Everyone in the club seemed to be the most beautiful people either of them had ever seen. Carter found his eye wandering as they made their way through the crowd. The thick shapes of the Rio women enticed Carter, and the fact that they were scantily dressed left nothing to his imagination.

Miamor laughed and said, "See, I told you that you would have a good time."

They found a table and a waitress brought them a round of drinks. "*Hola, Americanos,*" she greeted with a smile.

Every waitress in the place served in boy shorts and bra, but the one who served them made the uniformed look seem erotic. Her breasts popped out of the bra, sitting perky and high, and her flat stomach was flaw- less. Her wide hips were accompanied by a beautiful behind.

"My name is Lucy and I'll be serving you tonight. This first round of tequila is on the house. Let me know if I can get you anything else," she said. Her accent was exotic and her dark hair gave her a mysterious look.

"You need to loosen up!" Miamor shouted over the music. "Drink up!"

Carter and Miamor hit a shot of tequila, and then Carter ordered cognac as Miamor indulged in her cocktail.

"You want to try it?" she asked, nodding at the dance floor.

"Nah, ma, you know my movements don't change much. I don't do the two-stepping thing. Go ahead though. I'll enjoy the view," he said as he leaned into her ear.

As Lucy placed their third round of drinks on the table, she smiled and asked, "You guys aren't going to dance?"

Carter shook his head.

"You have to, *papi!* Do you know how many American men run away down here just to visit this very club?" Lucy exclaimed as she stood with her hand on her hip.

"I'll pass, ma," he said with a smile.

"I guess that's easy for you to do with a girlfriend like this," Lucy said as she winked at Miamor. "How about you? You no dance?"

Miamor shrugged and Lucy shook her head. "Oh no! *Mamacita,* you are too pretty to be a wall flower," she said.

Lucy grabbed Miamor's hand and pulled her to her feet. "Can I borrow her?" Lucy asked. "Please, *papi!* I promise I will bring her back in one piece."

Carter waved his hand and sat in the cut as he watched Miamor be pulled onto the dance floor with Lucy as her partner.

"What do I do?" Miamor asked.

"You let me seduce you, *mami.* Just relax and have a good time. The little pill I put in your drinks will have you rolling in no time," Lucy whispered in her ear.

Miamor's mind numbed as Lucy circled her like a predator. Her nipples hardened, and Lucy pulled her close. Her breath caught in her throat as Lucy's hands roamed all over Miamor's body, leaving a tingle every place that she touched.

"You're a very pretty girl. He is lucky to have you," Lucy whispered in her ear as she planted a wet kiss on her neck.

Miamor's mind spun and everything felt good. Her entire body tingled, ached, begged to be touched. She had never popped Ecstasy before, but now that it had been slipped to her, she enjoyed the ride. "Did you give him some?" Miamor asked as she glanced over at her man.

"I did, *mami,* and I usually don't partake in the club's activities, but as soon as you two sat down in my section I knew that I wanted to suck the sweetness out of your pussy while you suck on his black dick," Lucy whispered.

Miamor's eyes popped open, and it was then that she realized that she had even closed them. Lucy's words made her panties wet, and she moaned helplessly. She had never been so horny in her life.

"I bet his dick is big, eh?" Lucy asked. "Tell me it's big, *mami.*"

"It's big." Miamor panted as Lucy grinded on her to the slow beat of the music. Her hands were planted on Miamor's hips as she aligned their pussies, grinding and winding slowly.

"I want to suck that black dick. Can I suck his dick, mama?" the Latina asked.

Under normal circumstances Miamor would have cut the girl's tongue out of her mouth, but Miamor was in the moment. The overwhelming desire that she felt made her consider sharing Carter with the voluptuous South American vixen. It was every man's fantasy to bring another woman into his bed with wifey, and Miamor smirked as she thought, *That just might happen tonight.*

Carter leaned back in the booth and felt his dick jump as he watched Miamor dance with Lucy. Undoubtedly they were the two most beautiful women in the club, and the steamy session they were having on the dance floor had Carter on brick. He ordered a cigar, and a pure Cuban was brought out for him. He clipped the end and held it up to the flame that a waitress held for him. All the while his eyes never left the show Miamor was putting on for him.

Their eyes locked, and Carter exhaled a mouthful of smoke. He nodded for her to return to the table, and Miamor obliged, bringing Lucy back with her.

"That was quite a performance, ma," Carter said as he licked his lips. The way he did it told Miamor that he wanted to lick another set of lips as well, and she smiled.

"Why don't we head back," she said.

Carter stood to his feet and Miamor added, "All three of us."

Momentarily thrown off kilter, Carter paused. He didn't know if this was a trick or if he had heard her wrong.

"When in Rome, right?" she asked again with a mischievous smile. Carter loved the spontaneity of it all. He would have never asked her for a threesome, but he for damn sure wasn't going to turn one down at her suggestion.

Carter grabbed Miamor's hand, and Miamor grabbed Lucy's hand as they left the club and entered their awaiting car.

"Back to the villa," Carter instructed as he rolled up the window that separated them from the curious eyes of the driver.

As soon as their privacy was official, Miamor lowered her head into Carter's lap, releasing his already hard penis.

"Oooh, *papi!*" Lucy moaned as she admired his size. Carter sat back in the seat as Miamor pushed Lucy's head down onto Carter's dick. Carter gasped as Lucy's mouth took him in.

"Oh shit," he whispered as she went to work.

Miamor kissed his lips and whispered in his ear, "This is going to be the best night of your life."

He gripped the back of her head, intensifying their kiss as he clenched his ass and fucked Lucy's mouth at the same time. Her head game was out of this world as she topped him off, licking and sucking his dick.

"Scoot down, *papi*," she whispered as she pulled him off the edge of the seat. There was something about the way she called him *papi* that made Carter want to cum in her mouth, and when he felt her tongue dip in his ass he moaned out loud.

"You like that, baby?" Miamor whispered. Miamor lowered her head and went south on her man as she sucked his dick while Lucy licked his ass. Carter felt as if he would explode at any moment. He placed his hand on the back of Miamor's head and sucked his teeth.

"Psss, damn, ma. Suck that shit," he groaned. Carter had hit a lot of women in his day, but he had never had a session this good. He had no idea that it was the E taking him to new heights.

The nut that built up inside of him finally erupted, and Miamor locked eyes with him as she swallowed every drop. She and Lucy arose as the car stopped moving.

"Let's take this inside. I'm not done with you yet," Miamor said. He had never seen her so uninhibited, and he liked it.

The threesome adjusted their clothing and then rushed into the villa. The women couldn't keep their hands off of Carter as they fumbled to get him out of his clothes. Carter kissed Miamor passionately and pulled back suddenly. "You got any condoms?"

Miamor shook her head because they didn't use them with one another, but she wasn't so high as to let another bitch sample her dick without protection.

"I have them," Lucy whispered as she removed a Magnum from her purse. She ripped it open and slid it onto Carter's dick. It was hard, as if the first nut had never even happened. The softness of her hands made him close his eyes as Lucy began to stroke his dick gently.

Carter turned Miamor around and pulled his hardness away from Lucy. He slid into Miamor from behind, standing in the middle of the room, and gripped her hips so that she had nowhere to run.

Lucy loved the sight and couldn't feel left out for long. She got on her knees in front of Miamor and parted the petals of her delicate flower.

"Oh my goodness!" Miamor yelled in pleasure when she felt Lucy's mouth on her clit. The dick Carter was serving from behind and the ecstasy that Lucy provided in front threw Miamor into a frenzy. Her body shook, having earthquakes of pleasure as the pair pleased her. She scared herself because she loved this threesome so much she knew that she would definitely try it again, and next time it wouldn't be only for Carter.

Lucy folded her lips over her teeth and bit down on Miamor's clit, feasting on the juicy piece of flesh until Miamor could no longer take it.

"Eat it! Please, keep going, Lucy. Oh shit, Carter! Oh, Carter!" Miamor screamed.

"Cum for me, ma . . . let her taste it," Carter whispered. His deep baritone in her ear pushed Miamor off the cliff, and she enjoyed the free fall as she dove into a sea of orgasms. Her eyes rolled in the back of her head, and Lucy backed up as Carter bent Miamor over onto the arm of the couch.

He stroked her deep and at a rapid pace until finally he exploded.

The threesome fucked all over the villa, going round after round. Miamor fucked Carter, Carter fucked Lucy, Lucy fucked Miamor, and every other combination possible. They all lowered their inhibitions for the sake of animalistic desires. They simply wanted to please and be pleased for the night. Finally exhaustion plagued them, and Lucy fell asleep in the couple's bed as Miamor and Carter lay in each other's arms.

"Did we really just do that?" Miamor asked with a laugh.

Carter nodded as he turned toward her and brushed the hair from her face. "Do you regret it?" he asked.

Miamor shook her head. "No, as long as you enjoyed it as much as I did, then I don't regret any of it. You're my man and my king. Every king deserves to have a concubine every once in a while." Miamor winked at him and reached up to kiss his lips. "I'll do anything for you, Carter. For forgiving me and taking me back into your life, I will do all that I can to make you happy."

"You don't have to do anything, Miamor. This was good, but this isn't you, ma. Don't get me wrong—I enjoyed it. I more than enjoyed it, but you don't have to do anything extra. Just by ringing my doorbell on a rainy night you made the rest of my life a happy one. Now get some sleep," Carter said. He kissed her forehead and closed his eyes, positive that at the moment there wasn't a man on earth in a better position than he.

Chapter 11

"I guess he wasn't the good twin after all."
—Miamor

Carter leaned over and kissed Miamor's forehead and then took one last look at the lovely Lucy as they both slept peacefully, legs intertwined sexily with each other. Carter shook his head as he recalled the steamy sex session from the previous night. He tapped Lucy's thigh, stirring her from her slumber.

"Hmm . . . Morning, *papi*," she whispered as she reluctantly rolled over to face him.

Down boy, he thought as his dick jumped from the way she addressed him. He smirked and she crawled on all fours. "You like it when I call you *papi?*" she asked seductively.

"Time to get dressed, ma. Playtime's over," he said. "And be careful not to wake her." He motioned toward Miamor as Lucy nodded in compliance.

He walked out of the bedroom, giving Lucy some privacy. He walked to the spare bedroom and opened the closet. It looked like a military arsenal inside. He removed two handguns and put them into his shoulder holsters. He placed one in his waistline. He didn't anticipate a problem with Buttons. They had done business amicably for too long for anything to go wrong, but he never went anywhere without his strap. It was just another accessory for him.

He wrote a note for Miamor and placed it on the kitchen counter.

"Hmm-hmm."

Lucy cleared her throat behind him and he turned around to face her. He pulled his Armani leather wallet out of his pocket and removed a card.

"Last night was good, *papi*. Anytime you and your girlfriend are in Rio, please look me up. I'd love to see both of you again," she whispered as she stood close to him, so close that he smelled the peppermint on her breath.

Carter handed her the card. "You call that number and my man will take care of you. Five thousand dollars for the night."

Lucy's eyes widened in surprise. "I'm not a hooker."

"I never implied that, sweetheart, but those tips you're getting at the club can't possibly take you very far. Accept the money on behalf of me and my lady. For the good time you showed us last night," he replied.

"Wow, *papi*," she replied. "That girl in there really is lucky. I hope she knows."

"Nah, I'm the lucky one," Carter answered. He extended his arm for her to walk out in front of him, and they headed for the door.

His driver was standing attentively out front. "My driver will take you anywhere you need to go," Carter said.

Lucy smiled and bid farewell to Carter as he watched her get into the car. He waited until it pulled away before he signaled for one of the local cabbies who sat along the street.

Carter's mind immediately shifted to business as he entered the shabby vehicle. He gave directions to Buttons' home as he sat low while the speed of the cab caused the streets to fly by in a blur.

As the cab drew closer to Buttons' private estate, the cab driver spoke up. "I didn't even know this road existed until a few weeks ago, and now this is the second time I've come here. You Americans must know something we don't," he said.

Carter frowned as he sat up in his seat. No one knew of Buttons' whereabouts except for The Cartel. This spot practically didn't exist, so the fact that the cabbie had been there before alarmed Carter.

"You say you've been here before? Recently?" he asked.

Carter could see Buttons' home in the near distance as the cab hobbled down the extremely bumpy, under-developed road.

"Yeah, another American came here a while back. A bigshot from Miami. He tipped me a pretty penny. Isn't that what you Americans say?"

Carter reached in his holster and removed a pistol as he cocked it, suddenly feeling as though he had eyes on him. He looked around him, feeling threatened.

"Yo, my man. Do you remember the man's name that you drove out here?" Carter asked.

"Oh *sí*, senor! He was the money man! Money was his name," the cab driver stated.

As soon as the words filled the air, bullets filled the car. The rear windshield shattered as bullets flew, causing glass to rain down over him.

"Fuck!" Carter yelled out as he ducked in the back seat. "Drive!"

The cab driver didn't move as Carter pointed his gun out of the back of the car and fired.

BANG! BANG! BANG!

A van of three gunmen had pulled up behind him. His 9 mms were no match for the rapid blasts of the AK-47s of Buttons' goons. He was a sitting duck.

He turned to encourage the driver to go, but quickly discovered that the man was slumped over the steering wheel. Carter busted back, using his marksman aim, but the way the car was being Swiss cheesed, he knew that it wouldn't be long before one of the bullets would deliver his end.

Sweat covered his brow as he threw his gun in frustration after emptying the clip.

TAT! TAT! TAT! TAT! TAT! TAT!

He removed another pistol and let it spit as he pushed open the back door of the cab. As soon as he crawled out, a biting burn penetrated his left shoulder.

"Agh!" he shouted as the blast sent him flying backward, flooring him. He lay perfectly still as blood flooded from the wound in his shoulder. He bit his inner jaw as pain seared through him, but he lay still.

The firing stopped as the men spoke in Spanish. One of them approached, and Carter heard the footsteps crunching against the dirt as they drew near. His finger was already wrapped around the trigger of his gun as he lay with his eyes closed.

The other two goons stayed back as their comrade went to check Carter's status. The goon stood over him, seeing the blood that now covered Carter's entire shirt. Carter held his breath, not wanting to give away the fact that he was alive.

"He's dead!" the goon called out.

Carter prayed that Buttons' men weren't as thorough as his own. Zyir or any of his other goons would have put a bullet in his head just for good measure, just to make sure that the job was done. Luckily for him, this did not happen.

"Let's get out of here!" he heard one of them call out as the goon standing over him rushed back to the escape van. Carter waited until the he heard the van pull away before he rolled over onto his side.

Groaning and in extreme pain, he heaved as he leaned against the cab. He was soaked in his own blood and feared the worst. He struggled to his feet and then pulled open the driver's door.

"Arghh!" he roared as the pain in his shoulder vibrated throughout his entire body. He pulled the driver out and left his dead body in the dirt as he got into the bullet-riddled car, skirting off at full speed as he raced back to Miamor.

***

Miamor slowly came out of the sex- and drug-induced fog as she opened her eyes. The bed was empty and the room bright as the sun blared through the open windows. She could smell the salty ocean coming in with the breeze and she sat up, groggily, as she meandered to her feet.

"Carter!" she called as she walked out of the bedroom. She half expected to find him sexing Lucy on the living room balcony. *I'd kill him,* she thought with a laugh, shaking her head because she knew that her jealousy over her man would rear its ugly head sooner or later. She found the entire villa empty and then went into the kitchen. Her mouth was extremely dry and as she opened the refrigerator she finally noticed the note that Carter had left. It was placed underneath a 45 mm pistol. She smiled as she moved the gun and picked up the letter.

> Gone to handle business. Be back shortly. I love you.
>
> –C

Miamor crumbled the note in her hand and poured herself a glass of orange juice before retreating to the bathroom. Suddenly she felt hot and her mouth watered as vomit tickled the back of her throat. She lunged for the toilet and buried her head inside as she keeled over, her insides erupting. *What the fuck is wrong with me? What did Lucy give me last night?* she thought as her stomach clenched and she vomited again. Miamor breathed heavily as she closed her eyes and stood.

She leaned over the sink to rinse out her mouth, then headed for the shower. She turned on the water and tested it, placing her hands underneath the stream before she stepped inside. The rain showerhead was soothing as she closed her eyes and enjoyed the tiny beads of water that massaged her entire body as they fell upon her.

Her body felt alive after last night's rendezvous, and she shook her head as she opened her mouth, inviting the water to rinse away her sins. When Miamor opened her eyes, a shadow danced on the door of the bathroom, followed by a creak of the hardwood floor. She swiped her hand across her face and looked again, but nothing was there except for the blowing sheer curtain that covered the window.

Miamor's heart thumped rapidly inside of her chest. She had lived years of this paranoia, watching over her shoulder, thinking everyone was out to get her. She saw ghosts when no one was there, but in her years of being in the game she learned one thing: to always follow her gut.

Miamor slid out of the back of the shower curtain but left the water running as she hid behind the door. She knew that it couldn't be Carter. He knew her checkered past. He would have announced himself before sneaking up on her.

She winced when she thought about the gun that she had left lying on the kitchen counter. She would have to do this the hard way. She picked up the porcelain cover to the toilet and waited behind the door. She felt foolish after a minute passed and nothing happened.

Am I tripping? she thought.

When she heard the door creak open, she knew that she was on point. A masked man entered the bathroom quietly, moving with the stealth of a clumsy-ass giant. If he thought he would catch her slipping, he had another think coming. Compared to her murder game, this goon was an amateur, or at least he moved like one.

Miamor knew that he had an advantage over her because he was armed and twice her size. She waited, and just as he reached for the shower curtain she charged him. She lifted the heavy top over her head.

"Agh!" she yelled from her gut as she brought it crashing down over his head. She lifted her foot and kicked him in his back, sending his him flying into the bathtub. He fell clumsily inside as the gun fell from his hand. Miamor had no time to reach for it as the man fumbled out of the tub. She saw his hand wrap around the gun, and she closed the shower curtain, blocking his view as she darted for the window.

BANG! BANG! BANG!

She dove headfirst out of the window as the glass tore through her skin and she fell fifteen feet to the sandy beach below. She hit the ground hard, knocking the wind from her lungs. She staggered to her feet as she looked around, her vision slightly blurry from hitting her head.

Shaking the stars from her eyes, she gripped the side of the house as she ran up the back stairs that led directly to the kitchen. She raced to the gun that lay on the counter and gritted her teeth as she saw red. She cocked the pistol, and just as she stepped toward the bathroom, the goon came stumbling out. She aimed.

BOOM! BOOM!

She hit him with two shots—one in the head and one in the heart. He dropped to his knees then landed face first into the hardwood floor.

"Bitch-ass nigga," she mumbled as she stepped over his dead body and went into the bedroom. She quickly threw on her clothes from the night before. She moved as fast as she could until Carter's voice boomed through the villa.

"Miamor!" he yelled.

She rushed out to him. "Carter!" she gasped when she saw that he was bloody. She covered the room in a flash as he gripped his shoulder in agony.

"I'm fine!" he shouted urgently. "We've got to get out of here now. Grab the passports. Get a gun and let's go."

Miamor took instruction well and didn't freeze under pressure. She sprang into action, gathering their belongings and two handguns. She also grabbed anything that looked as if it could help her stop Carter's bleeding before they exited the villa. Carter's driver opened the door in alarm.

"To the airstrip as quickly as possible," Carter instructed.

✳✳✳

Zyir sat at the kitchen table as he watched Breeze cook.

"I love the way you move, ma," he said as she turned toward him. He smiled, causing her to blush.

"Oh yeah?" she asked as she sashayed over to her husband. "I love that you love it," she responded. He opened his legs and pulled Breeze into his space as she bent to kiss his lips. His hands slid up her dress.

DING! DONG!

The doorbell rang and he groaned, knowing that whoever had visited had interrupted their flow.

"You expecting anyone?"

Breeze shook her head and removed her apron as she went toward the front entrance. "It's probably Leena. I haven't heard from her much since she moved out, but some of her stuff is still here. Maybe she's coming to pick it up," Breeze said.

"Tell Leena to call first next time!" Zyir said with a wink.

Breeze chuckled as she pulled open the door.

"Money!" she exclaimed. She opened her arms for a hug. "Hey! What's up?"

Money smiled at the sight of Breeze. He truly loved and worshipped the ground that his sister walked on. Ever since they were children he had always protected her. Now she stood, the image of beauty in front of his face. She reminded him so much of their mother that it was uncanny.

He had gotten the call from Buttons that the execution was a success, so he was coming over to be with his sister. He knew that she would take the news hard when the phone call of Zyir's death came in. He expected it at any moment.

"You gonna leave me out here on your doorstep?" he asked playfully, holding out his hands as he looked around.

"No, of course not. Come in. Me and Zy were just about to sit down to eat. You want to stay for dinner?" she asked.

"Zy?" Monroe questioned, confused. "I thought Zyir was in Rio."

Zyir suddenly walked into the room. "Change of plans. Carter went in my place," Zyir stated.

Monroe's face drained of all color as his eyes widened in alarm.

"Why didn't anyone tell me?" he asked.

Zyir frowned and noticed that Monroe appeared worried. "Why would anyone need to tell you?" he asked.

"I've got to get out of here. I forgot I've got a late meeting," Monroe stammered as he backed out of the house.

"A meeting? At nine o'clock at night?" Zyir grilled.

Monroe shifted uncomfortably in his stance, feeling transparent as if Zyir could see the guilt resting on his shoulders. "You a'ight?" Zyir asked as he stepped to Monroe suspiciously, placing one hand on Monroe's shoulder.

Monroe shrugged Zyir's hand off and stared him in the eyes. Breeze watched the tense moment in confusion. Neither Zyir nor Monroe broke the hard stare.

"Zyir," Breeze called his name. "Monroe!" Breeze shouted once she saw that there was an obvious beef between the two men she loved. "What is going on? What are you two not telling me? What is wrong?" she demanded as she looked back and forth between them.

Zyir stepped back, allowing his wife to separate him from Monroe. "Nothing's wrong, baby girl. Right, Monroe? Everything's good in our camp? No snake niggas calling plays or no shit like that? Monroe Diamond." His voice was accusatory and his glare no nonsense as he stood his ground, his hands folded in front of him as he emphasized each word with a head nod in Monroe's direction.

The way Zyir stared at him made Monroe's temper flare and his conscience as well. He was eager to get out of the house and make a call to Buttons. He had unknowingly given the green light for Carter, his flesh and blood, to be murdered.

"Everything's good, Breeze," Monroe said. He leaned in and kissed his sister's cheek and then walked off, obviously stressed.

Breeze stood back and folded her arms as she cocked her neck to the side. "What was that?" she asked.

"Leave it alone," Zyir snapped as he stormed off, retreating to his study.

***

Carter was silent as Miamor nursed his wound as best she could. They were thirty thousand feet in the air and she was far from a doctor, but she managed to slow down his bleeding.

"Does it hurt?" she asked sympathetically.

"I'll be fine, ma. Don't worry yourself. I just need to get back to Miami as soon as possible," Carter said as his thoughts drifted to his disloyal brother.

"Who did this?" Miamor asked.

"Monroe," Carter replied.

Miamor saw Mecca's face flash before her eyes. "I guess he wasn't the good twin after all," she whispered. She kissed his cheek and took her seat as Carter grunted an inaudible response.

After taking Mecca's life, he knew that taking Monroe's was not something that he wanted to do.

"It's time to settle all scores," Carter said as he grabbed Miamor's hand. "Yours as well. I'm calling a meeting and we are going to settle this once and for all. I'm tired of the treachery tearing this family apart."

"So you're going to forgive him?" Miamor asked.

"Didn't I forgive you?" he responded.

Chapter 12

"Today we are each other's judge,
jury, and executioner."

—Carter

Miamor sat at the table terrified as the eyes of the Diamond family burned holes through her. Never in her life had she felt so persecuted. It was if she had a scarlet letter burnt into her forehead. The family was divided, and she knew that she was a big part of the turmoil, if not the cause itself. She felt naked, like a deer in hunting season, as she sat next to Carter. A 9 mm would have put her mind at ease, but she had promised Carter that she would give up that lifestyle. She had to play the role of wifey and as such, she had to allow him to be her protector. Old habits died hard, however, and Miamor's trigger finger twitched against the table as she kept a stone face while staring straight ahead.

Carter placed his hand on her thigh beneath the table and gave it a gentle squeeze, reassuring her that she was safe. As long as she was sitting next to him, no one dared to harm her, but it didn't put her mind at ease. Considering that Monroe had sent goons at Carter in Rio, it let her know that he wouldn't even blink at the thought of killing her. She inhaled deeply as Carter stood. His arm was bandaged and in a sling; his anger was etched in a grimace on his handsome face.

"Our empire is in jeopardy. We've faced a lot of adversaries over the years—the Haitians, the drug cartel out of Mexico—and we're still here. We're still standing, but we won't be for long if we don't air out our grievances. There is nothing worse than a snake in the grass. Deceit within our own organization is the only thing that will make The Cartel fall. We each have our own sins that we have committed over the years. The game doesn't allow you to make it this far without having some regrets. Those secrets are our greatest threat. We have to keep The Cartel strong or the little niggas lurking and preying will tear us apart. If there is one crack, one weak link, the entire team will fall," Carter said as he walked around the table, addressing his loved ones.

"I have built a power circle. Everyone at this table is family. I trust each one of you with my life. So in turn, you should trust each other with your lives. There can be no treachery among us, so today we are going to air everything out. We're going to lay all of our sins on the table. Today we are each other's judge, jury, and executioner," Carter spoke seriously.

Silver platters lay in front of each person and were covered with a silver top. It appeared as though the table was set for a feast, and Carter nodded his head toward the display. "Lift the tops," he instructed.

Miamor lifted the top that lay in front of her, and her breath caught in her throat when she saw the pistol lying in front of her. Instinctively she reached on top of the table and checked the clip. It was full. Carter smirked, somewhat attracted as he watched her put one in the head and click off the safety before placing it back on the table.

"What is this, Carter? What's going on?" Breeze asked as she looked around the table in confusion.

"Breeze, in order to trust one another, we have to admit the things that we've done. Let the person without sin cast the first stone," Carter said.

"Or bullet," Zyir added as he stood to his feet. "I'm thorough. Admission of our sins, right?" he asked rhetorically. "I'll go first. This has been on my chest for a long time." He looked down at Breeze and she smiled at him reassuringly, confident that no matter what came out of his mouth she would still love him. Zyir was like the sun to Breeze. Her world revolved around him. She gave him a wink, and Zyir turned to his captive audience and spoke. "The day that Breeze was kidnapped was my fault. I got caught slipping. Carter told me to look after her, and instead of protecting her I . . . entertained her. We entertained each other. I was distracted and we were about to have sex when she was taken."

Monroe's jaw clenched as he stared at Zyir and watched his beautiful sister stand up by her man's side. The sight made his stomach turn. Their father would have rolled over in his grave if he knew Breeze was dating a man like Zyir. Big Carter always wanted the best for his children, and Zyir wasn't it.

"I don't blame him for what happened to me, so for any of you to would be wrong. We were young. We moved sloppy, but I'm here and I'm breathing and Ma'tee is dead," Breeze said, defending Zyir with conviction. "Those are skeletons that I buried a long time ago. That experience made me stronger. Nobody was to blame except for Ma'tee and the bitches that helped him take me . . ."

"And me," Miamor spoke up. Her voice shook as she stood to her feet. Her eyes filled with tears as she looked around the room. Her bottom lip quivered as she reached for the gun. "What I'm about to tell you will not be easy to swallow, and I've never let bullets fly my way without busting back, so you can either take what I'm about to say peacefully or this can get very ugly."

She looked unsurely at Carter, and he nodded his head for her to continue. The more she exposed her true self, the more infatuated with her he became. She was a gangster. Her only fault was that she had been commissioned by his enemy to take down his family. That he could forgive, because now she was by his side and the way she moved he knew that if needed she would be an asset. He hoped she never had to come off the bench, but if she had to, she could and would. That alone endeared her to Carter. As his eyes scanned the room, he realized that he would let no judgment come her way. If he could look past her flaws, everyone else would have to as well.

She looked at Breeze sincerely and took a deep breath. "The women who helped snatch you the night you were kidnapped were my friends. We were a part of a group called The Murder Mamas. Ma'tee paid us to kill the leaders of The Cartel," she said.

As soon as the words left her mouth, she had two weapons aimed directly at her. Zyir and Monroe both held their positions, standing, arms extended, guns ready to pop off in her direction.

Miamor had anticipated their anger, and her own gun was pointed back at them, going back and forth between Monroe and Zyir.

"Let her finish," Breeze said as she stood to her feet, pressing her hands firmly against the table as she stared across at Miamor. "I want to know why!"

Miamor swallowed the lump in her throat as she continued. "Because he paid us to. I wasn't there that night, but I did know that they were determined to get to The Cartel. By that time I had already fallen in love with your brother. I told them I was out, but they took it upon themselves to still work with Ma'tee."

"You've got this bitch around us like she's family after what she did?" Zyir asked as he looked at Carter.

"Lower your pistols," Carter said.

"Let her finish. That's not all, is it? There's more to the fucking story, right, ma?" Monroe asked. "You were hired to take out our family, ruin The Cartel. I've heard about The Murder Mamas, so I know that you didn't fail. So who else did you get at? Which one of my family members is in a shallow grave because of you?" Monroe grilled.

"It's more complicated than that. I didn't just point and shoot your family. Your brother Mecca. We tried to set him up. He sniffed us out and killed my sister in a hotel. After that it became personal. I got caught up in a game with him. I wanted him dead. I hated him for taking her away from me. So I gunned for his head, but I never got the opportunity to catch him until I saw him at the memorial that was thrown for Breeze when you all thought she was dead. I was a guest of Carter's, and he slipped me a drink that I gave to your mother. Mecca tried to poison me, but ended up watching his own mother drink what was intended for me," she admitted. Tears of regret flowed down her face. "Your mother was the only innocent life I have ever taken."

Breeze picked up her gun as Monroe pulled back the hammer of his.

"Lower your pistols," Carter said, trying to intervene.

"We can't just shoot her," Leena said as she stood to her feet, holding her son in her arms. "Monroe, our son is here!" she protested as she looked around the room in distress. "Carter, stop this. Do something!"

Carter came off his hip with a chrome .45 automatic. "I said lower your fucking guns," Carter shouted angrily. "If you judge her, you judge yourselves. You judge me! Hold up a mirror and think about the things that you've done. What betrayal have you brought to the table? What about Leena, Money? Huh? You fucked Mecca's bitch. He was your brother and he loved her! He loved her so much that he shot you over her! That entire situation started a war between us and Ma'tee! A war that almost crippled us! And what about that play you just put down in Rio?"

Carter's tone lowered as he stared intently at Monroe. He saw a glint of recognition in Monroe's eyes, and that was all it took to confirm that Monroe had plotted against his own team. He stepped so close to Monroe that he was whispering in his ear. What he was about to say no one else in the room needed to hear. "Fuck was you thinking?" he grilled through clenched teeth, unable to contain his anger. He kept it moving, but both men knew that it was a conversation that they would have soon.

"Zy! What about you? You want to add up bodies? Huh? I know what your murder count look like, fam! Even I'm not without guilt. I killed our brother. I shot Mecca while he was praying at an altar for forgiveness."

Carter's emotion was written all over his tortured face as he advocated for Miamor, and upon his confession Monroe broke down as well. He turned his gun on Carter, forgetting all about Miamor. Breeze and Zyir dropped their weapons.

"He was my brother!" Monroe shouted.

"And you were mine!" Carter yelled back. "I thought he killed you! I thought he went against the family. If he could draw on you and lie about it, I knew that he would eventually betray me. I made a choice! In your honor, Monroe! I took a life! For my brother! The same way she took lives for her sister! The same way you are

ready to take my life for Mecca! Forgiveness, brother,"
Carter said, heaving from the adrenaline that was
racing through him. "That is what we are here for. This
is the only family we have left. Let's solidify it. Let's
expand."

Miamor stood, holding her belly as she thought of
the child that grew inside of her. She was carrying
Carter's seed, and as long as it had a small part of him,
she knew that it would be special. Carter was the greatest man she had ever met, and as she looked at him she
felt pride in being his woman.

As Miamor admired Carter, Breeze studied her. She
saw the undeniable connection that Miamor had with
her brother. There was a glow about her that Breeze
recognized.

"You're pregnant," Breeze whispered, her own tears
building in her eyes.

Miamor's neck snapped to the right to look at Breeze,
and Carter looked down at Miamor in shock. Miamor
had not even told him yet and somehow Breeze knew.
Miamor nodded her head as the gun she now held at
her side slipped from her fingers and clattered loudly
as it hit the floor. "I am," she admitted emotionally as
she held up her hands. "And now I'm defenseless. No
gun, no weapons, no motives. You can kill me now if
you want, but I want you to know that I am so sorry for
the role I played in harming your family. I can't take
it back, but it is one of my life's biggest regrets. I love
your brother, Breeze. I love him with every part of me
and I want this baby . . . this life with him. I hurt you
and your family, but I would want nothing more than
to be a part of it now."

Breeze stared Miamor in the eyes and wished that
they had met under different circumstances. "I'm sorry
for the things that Mecca did to hurt you. I can still

see the loss in your eyes. I know how that feels. We all know how that feels. You are carrying my bloodline inside of you. No one at this table will do harm to you, Miamor. It's time to let bygones be bygones," Breeze said. She took her seat at the table and slid her gun to the center of the table, out of arm's reach.

"There's been enough loss in this family," Zyir said.

"You don't speak on this family," Monroe stated harshly.

"I am this family, homeboy," Zyir shot back. "I'm the family that took care of wifey and your seed while you were gone. So whether you like it or not, I'm here. I was here when you couldn't be."

Zyir took his seat and slid his gun to the center as well. Leena followed suit, pushing the weapon in front of her away in disgust. She was in over her head. She had never been more than arm candy for one of the Diamond men. She didn't know anything about this side of their lives. She just wanted to restore normalcy and peace into their lives, and if it meant accepting Miamor, she was all for it.

"Forgiveness, Monroe," Carter stated. He put his gun on the table and walked toward his brother, hands up, until he was directly in front of Monroe. He was so close that Money's gun was pressed into his chest, directly over his heart. He felt Money's hand begin to tremble. "If you sit down at this table, then we let go of the past and work toward building our future. If not, then pull the trigger now and let it be known where you stand."

Monroe lowered his head in turmoil. The entire room was an emotional mess. Everyone except Zyir was a wreck. He kept his composure, his hand near his hip where his extra pistol rested. He anticipated Monroe's every move. If his finger moved an inch, Zyir was prepared to pop off. There was no way he was letting a nigga take Carter's life, brother or not.

Monroe's resolve melted as Carter wrapped his hand around Monroe's gun and removed it from his hand. Carter grabbed the back of Money's neck and pulled him in close as they both bowed their heads in silence.

"I love you, brother, and I'm sorry. Extend me your forgiveness, Money," Carter whispered in his ear. The way Carter spoke to him reminded Monroe so much of his father, taking him to an emotional place.

Monroe nodded his head and wiped his face with his hand while composing himself. "Forgiveness," he repeated. Carter could see the reluctance written all over Monroe.

Miamor breathed a sigh of relief as Carter returned to her side and everyone took their seats. A knock at the door sounded off, and Carter summoned in his chef.

"Now we break bread together as family," Carter said as his kitchen staff brought in a feast fit for a king. Wine was poured around the table, and Carter raised his glass.

"To The Cartel," he toasted.

Although tension still filled the room, everyone knew that this brought them one step closer to unity. They all raised their glasses in salute. "To The Cartel!"

Chapter 13

"Light that mu'fucka up."
— Monroe Diamond

Monroe sat through the dinner and was reserved as his thoughts worked overtime. He wasn't feeling the direction that The Cartel was being taken in. There was no honor among thieves. Carter had stolen Mecca's life and Zyir had stolen Monroe's identity. He wasn't feeling either of them too much at the moment. Carter would forever get a pass because he was family, but Zyir . . .

The only reason Monroe even conceded to the notion of forgiveness was because he was outnumbered at a table full of armed individuals. He had no wins in that circumstance. He wanted no part of any empire as long as Zyir was its leader. So he ate and drank, but rarely spoke as he readied his own troops for battle.

The clock struck midnight, and Leena leaned into him. "It's late. The baby is tired," she said.

He nodded toward the door. "You go ahead and let the driver take you home. I'll be there shortly. There are a few things I need to run by Carter and I don't want you waiting around," Monroe instructed. "My driver can drop you at your house, too, Breeze. I figure me, Carter, and Zyir have a lot to discuss."

Breeze turned to Zyir for confirmation. He nodded. "I guess that is good night then." Leena gathered her son's things as Breeze approached Miamor. "I want to sit down and talk with you whenever you have time for me," Breeze said.

Miamor nodded and Breeze gave her hand a gentle squeeze before walking out of the house. Leena followed suit.

Miamor kissed Carter's cheek and whispered in his ear, "I'll start clearing the table. I know we have a lot to talk about. I'm sorry I didn't tell you about the baby. You handle your business and we can talk as soon as everyone leaves."

She stood and removed his plate from in front of him.

"Let's take this to the sitting room," Carter said as he stood and led the way. The three men entered the room and an awkward silence fell among them.

"Now that we have all pulled down our skirts, can we get back to getting this money?" Zyir asked.

"I'm thinking along those same lines, but one thing has to change in order for me to be onboard with this," Monroe said.

"What's that?" Carter responded.

"Zyir is no longer head of my father's empire. Clearly his ties aren't strong enough to hold us down," Monroe said, speaking as if Zyir wasn't even in the room.

"I realize that you don't like me, Monroe, but don't speak about me like I'm a little-ass boy. I see through you, Money," Zyir said with a sarcastic chuckle. "You're like one of those little rich kids who thinks they're entitled to everything. You didn't even earn the spot you're begging for. You weren't in the thick of the war. You were off hiding somewhere, healing somewhere while we were here taking the shit to the streets. So miss me with the family speech. You hide behind that Diamond name like it's supposed to mean something to me. Miami has belonged to me for the past four years."

"Now isn't the time for change, Money," Carter said.

"There is never a good time for change," Monroe answered, his jaw tight. "We're blood. You and I both know that we should keep the power inside the family. It's how Papa would have wanted it."

"Look at this shit, Carter," Zyir scoffed as he shook his head disgracefully. "I can't get money with this nigga. You may let shit slide with him, but I'm not going to wait until the nigga put a bullet in me before I cut him off."

"Li'l nigga, I'll cut you off. You married into the power. Breeze is your only connection to this here. You don't got a bid in this circle," Monroe roared. He turned to Carter. "Your man either steps out of my father's seat or I'll make him. Ain't no compromising."

"Monroe, this is the snake shit that is putting holes in our ship. Think about what you're saying. Think about how you're moving. You thought I wouldn't find out that you were the one froze our connect with Buttons?" Carter asked. "I'm asking you, Monroe, to come on board. We need you, and there is a role to be played by each of us, equally important."

"As long as he's in then I'm out," Monroe said truthfully. "And you're without a connect. Meanwhile I'm plugged with Estes."

Carter knew that with Monroe's connection to his grandfather he couldn't be stopped. He was getting the bricks straight off the boat for next to nothing.

"The nigga's a snake, Carter. Fuck him. We don't need him," Zyir spat.

Monroe shook his head. He really didn't want to lose another brother. "You should have let this nigga go to Rio and it would have been taken care of. He would be a memory right now," Monroe finished.

Zyir shifted his stance and frowned. "What the fuck you say?" He approached Monroe.

Carter stepped out of the way, knowing that there was no point in standing between the two men. This confrontation had been brewing ever since Monroe's return. Carter leaned against the arm of his leather couch as he wiped his face with his hands, exasperated, as Zyir addressed Monroe.

"Fuck you say?" Zyir asked. Before he knew it his gun was out and he had Monroe yoked up with a pistol to his head.

"You might as well pull the trigger now because either way I'm going to put you in a grave for the disrespect," Monroe threatened as no fear passed through his eyes.

Carter shook his head. It was the first time in his life that he didn't know what to do. Usually he was calculating and sure in his ability to solve a problem, but in this situation he came up clueless. He watched his two brothers draw a line in the sand. It was at a point of no return. Guns had been drawn, threats had been made, truth had been revealed. Finally Carter spoke.

"This is my home, Zyir," he said.

"Another time and place then," Zyir sneered as he pushed Monroe away and backed down, keeping his gun in his hand, however. "Pussy-ass nigga."

Monroe chuckled as he adjusted his collar. "I tried to give you a chance on the strength of Carter, but you refuse to step down. Either you standing with me or against me, and anybody standing next to you can get it too," Monroe stated harshly. He looked at Carter. "You love my enemy, you become my enemy. So make your choice, brother. It's me or your man."

Carter was silent, but it was all the answer that Monroe needed. He wanted no indecisive players on his team.

"Then watch me burn The Cartel to the ground," Monroe said, his voice so full of hatred that it sent chills down Carter's spine. Monroe stormed out of the house and headed toward the cars that were lined up in front of Carter's home. He had already anticipated this feud, and his young wolves were just waiting for the orders. They sat curbside outside of Carter's mansion, guns loaded, eager to follow Monroe's lead. Monroe climbed into the first car and pulled out his phone to place a call.

"Light that mu'fucka up," he ordered.

He nodded his head for his goon to drive off and then listened as the carful of goons behind him unloaded their automatic assault rifles on Carter's mansion.

Bullets broke through every window as glass shattered everywhere and Zyir and Carter hit the floor.

"Get down!" Zyir yelled as he went to the window to try to bust back. He watched as Monroe's goons got into their cars and pulled off recklessly. He looked back at Carter bewildered.

"Miamor," he whispered. "Miamor!" Carter stood to his feet and ran toward the dining room. He sighed in relief as he saw her rising from the floor.

"Are you hit?" he asked as he patted her entire body, fearing the worst.

"I'm okay," she replied.

Zyir came into the room.

"I knew that he didn't mean it. I could see it in his eyes," Miamor said. "Money doesn't want to forgive, Carter. He wants war."

"Then that's what the nigga gon' get," Zyir interrupted.

Carter nodded his head, but his heart broke inside. He was caught in the middle of two men he would lay down his life for. He wished they could become one large circle of power, but Monroe couldn't see past his own ego trip. His jealousy had caused him to cross those who loved him. Carter knew what he had to do.

"Take care of him, but keep Breeze out of it," Carter replied.

"With pleasure," Zyir replied.

Chapter 14

"You are a part of our family now, Miamor.
There are no more secrets."
—Carter

Miamor waited for hours for Carter to come to bed, but he never showed. Minutes turned to hours and her eyes grew heavy. She thought of going to him, but knew that if he wanted her company he would have sought it. So she gave him space, giving him time to think as she hugged a pillow to her lonely body. She stared at the red numbers on the clock.

3:45 A.M.

She wished that he would talk to her, that he would confide in her. Carter undoubtedly had a lot on his mind, but so did she. She wanted to comfort him and in return to have his comfort.

She closed her eyes, giving into the exhaustion just as he walked into the room. The silhouette of her body could be seen from the doorway, and her light snores told him that she was asleep. He had brought her into his life thinking that they could settle down, when in actuality things were out of control. He crawled into bed beside her. The weight of him caused the bed to shift slightly, announcing his presence. Miamor turned to face him.

"Hey, stranger," she said.

"So you're having my baby, huh?" he asked.

"I am," she whispered. She touched his face and ran her thumb across his bushy eyebrows, taming them. She wondered what a child between the two of them would look like. "Is that a good thing?" she asked.

"That's the best thing, ma," he replied. "You are the only thing in my life that makes sense right now. How long have you known?"

"I suspected it in Rio. I was nauseated the morning after our big night. When we came back home I took a test. Needless to say it was positive," Miamor replied.

"You'll have the best of everything. The best doctors, the best insurance, the best care. I'll have Breeze help you with the arrangements," Carter said.

"I don't know if that's a good idea, Carter," Miamor replied hesitantly. After all the admissions of guilt Miamor just knew that Breeze would resent her.

"You are a part of our family now, Miamor. There are no more secrets. It will take time to heal all of our wounds, but this baby will bond the two of you. I know my sister. She has a very forgiving soul. She will do all that she can to help you bring her nephew into the world," Carter promised.

"Nephew, huh? How do you know it's not a girl?" she asked with a smirk.

"I make boys, ma . . . kings," he answered with a charming wink as he rolled on top of her. He kissed her passionately and slowly made his way south. He put her to sleep with an earth-shattering orgasm as the sun rose into the sky.

***

The atmosphere was unusually tense between Zyir and Breeze. He hadn't spoken a word to her since he returned from Carter's. She lay with her back against the headboard as she watched him put on his clothes.

"Zy," she said, breaking the silence. "What happened after I left last night?"

He didn't look her way as he grabbed his presidential Rolex off the dresser and slid it onto his wrist.

"I know something happened. What are you keeping from me?" she asked.

"Nothing, B, nothing happened," Zyir replied.

She heard the stress in his tone and knew that he was lying, but she didn't press the issue. When he was ready to talk to her about it he would. Zyir was her best friend, and there wasn't much that he kept from her. So she knew that once it became needed for her to know, then she would. Until then she dropped it. She rose from the bed; her silk Donna Karan pajamas hugged her slim frame.

"Well, whatever is bothering you, I hope it gets better," she said as she kissed his lips.

"I'm gonna go prepare breakfast," she said as she exited their bedroom.

Zyir sighed, his heart heavy as he sat on the edge of the bed. Beefing with Monroe was a lose/lose for him. If he murdered him, then he would break Breeze's heart, and if he let him live, then Monroe's jealousy would eventually be Zyir's downfall. He knew what had to be done; he just hated that it had come to this. There was enough money for everybody to eat, but Monroe wanted fame—or rather, infamy. He wanted to be the boss in an organization where one was not needed. So instead of getting to the money, they were embarking on war. A war between brothers—one that no matter who was left standing, everybody would lose.

***

Breeze sat in the middle of the crowded restaurant waiting patiently for Miamor to arrive. Accepting the woman who had torn her family apart was not an easy thing to do, but off the strength of Carter she was willing to try. The apparent bond that Miamor and Carter shared was deep, and Breeze knew that forgiving Miamor was the only option as long as she held the key to her brother's heart.

She sipped a mimosa as she looked around Breezes. She had owned the restaurant for years, and it was the only business that she made sure to maintain after her father's demise. He had purchased it for her, and Breeze felt like it was the only piece of him that she had left. It had survived through two wars, and Breeze smiled as she watched the busy patrons fraternizing around her establishment.

She smiled slightly as her mind drifted to better days, when adversaries and disloyalty didn't exist in her world. Now her world was corrupted. She sat toward the doors in public places to see who was coming and going. She felt wary at traffic lights when sandwiched between two cars. She carried a small handgun in the bottom of her handbag just in case she should need it. Breeze no longer lived under the veil of safety that her kingpin father had provided for her. She lived in a constant state of awareness at the fact that she now played her mother's role. She was the kingpin's wife.

She wondered if Taryn had ever felt so overwhelmed by her position. Her mother made life look so glamorous and effortless when she was alive. Breeze had no idea how her mother had pulled it off, but she hoped to learn to wear her crown just as gracefully.

Miamor walked through the door and Breeze's back stiffened. She scanned her enemy from head to toe. Breeze quickly saw Carter's money dripping off of Miamor. Not many women could rival Breeze's fashion sense, but Miamor proved to be a contender with the most expensive pair of Jimmy Choo heels from the upcoming fall collection gracing her feet. The Chanel bandage dress she wore showed every curve of her body, and Breeze gave the nod approval in her head. Miamor was wearing Carter's money well, that was for sure. She watched Miamor scan the crowd and take a deep breath as she finally spotted her. She tried to approach, but was halted by two large bodyguards who sat discreetly at the table beside Breeze's. She was taking no chances. Breeze had done her research on Carter's new girlfriend, and after having experienced so much destruction at her hands, she decided to move accordingly. Breeze sat as her bodyguard intercepted Miamor.

"Check her," Breeze said.

The bodyguards patted Miamor down and took a look inside her bag before allowing her access to Breeze.

"Have a seat," Breeze said as she motioned for the chair across from her.

Miamor rolled her eyes at Breeze's security measures then took her place at the table.

"I have to admit that I was surprised when I got your phone call," Miamor said.

"You're pregnant with my brother's child. I love Carter and I don't want to lose him. So we may as well get better acquainted," Breeze answered.

Her tone was chillier than Miamor appreciated. Usually Miamor took attitude from no one, but she knew that Breeze had earned the right to be displeased with her. She gave her a pass knowing that it was in her best interest to repair her relationship with the youngest member of the Diamond clan.

Miamor could teach Breeze a thing or two. If Miamor wanted to touch Breeze, the big bodyguards could have done nothing to stop her. Her girls would have had the scope on him before he could even check her Birkin.

Miamor motioned for one of the bodyguards to approach her. He leaned down toward her.

"You need to patrol the perimeter of the restaurant. Secure the inside before Breeze arrives and then put one at both entrances. If someone wants to get at her, by the time they get this close it's too late. They shouldn't even make it through the door," Miamor schooled.

The men looked toward Breeze for confirmation. She peered curiously at Miamor and then nodded her approval.

"Tips you picked up in your line of work?" Breeze commented snidely.

Miamor sighed and folded her hands across the table as she looked Breeze square in the eyes.

"I'm not in that life anymore, Breeze. I know you have a lot to hate me for, but I truly hope that we can be civil. I'm not perfect and I have a lot of skeletons in my closet. What I've done to you isn't half of the bad things that I've done, but targeting you and your family is my biggest regret. I love Carter, Breeze, and he loves you. I want us to get to a point where we can call ourselves acquaintances," Miamor said, hoping to establish an understanding with Breeze. She would love for things to be all rainbows and flowers with Breeze, but she wasn't naïve. Breeze would need time to get over all of Miamor's past transgressions.

Breeze was silent for a moment as she tapped the bottom of her champagne flute with her blue manicured nail. Miamor couldn't read her, and she smiled at the fact that Breeze Diamond had grown up. She wasn't as green as she had been upon the very first meeting. Life had caused her to transform from a girl into a beautiful young woman, with limitless power in her hands.

"Have you chosen a doctor yet?" Breeze asked out of the blue.

Miamor shook her head. "Carter suggested that I ask you to help with that," Miamor said.

"You'll meet with our family doctor. I'll make the arrangements for you," Breeze offered. "I can't help but be excited about your pregnancy. This family needs some new blood in it. Maybe a child can restore the purity in our lives."

Breeze beckoned for the waitress and then said, "And just so you know, I forgive you. We don't have to discuss anything that has happened in the past ever again. As long as you make Carter happy, then I'm happy. Treat him well."

Miamor nodded. She was grateful for Breeze's kind heart. There was no way that Miamor could have done the same if the shoe was on the other foot. "I will. And thank you."

"It's nothing," Breeze responded. A huge smile spread across her lips. "Now let's talk baby names."

Chapter 15

"It was like Mecca's ghost
flew into that nigga."
—Fly Boogie

Monroe took to the streets the way a duck took to water, and he made no apologies for his brute way of ruling. He had already set up shop in all of The Cartel's most profitable territories, but instead of sharing blocks, he was taking them over. Monroe pulled up to Zyir's most profitable trap and exited the car with his goon squad in tow. Fly Boogie stood up and saluted Monroe.

"What's good, boy?" he greeted.

Monroe was stone faced as he removed his gun from his waistline and popped Fly Boogie without remorse. The young kid folded like a lawn chair as the hot lead fired from Monroe's gun filled his belly. Monroe was on some terminating shit. Anyone who rocked with Zyir was a threat and on his list to be laid down.

He ascended the steps and knocked on the door in the rhythm that allowed him entry. His goons stood on the sides of the door, out of the view of anyone who looked out of the peephole. When they saw that it was Monroe, he was given access and welcomed inside, but when they saw the niggas with burners who came in after him they quickly regretted the decision.

Gunfire erupted, and a complete massacre occurred as Monroe stood and watched his team put in work. They were so thorough they only delivered head shots. No vest in the world could protect against a hollow to the dome, and that's what he trained his mob to deliver. All five men in the trap were executed, and the cook-up queens were tied up ass naked. Monroe smoked a cigar, enjoying the feel of the smoke in his lungs as he paced up and down the line of women. They squirmed and cried as they tried to free themselves from their constraints. As he paced, he poured gasoline from the can in his hand. The stench of the liquid filled the room as he doused the women.

"This is the price you pay when you work for Zyir," Monroe stated. He handed the gas can off to one of his goons and then pulled the cigar from his mouth. He looked at it as he blew a cloud of smoke from his mouth, and then he flicked the cigar onto the line of women. Flames instantly erupted and howls of immeasurable pain sounded out in the apartment.

"Let's go," Monroe ordered. He noticed that his squad had bagged up the money and the product that they had found in the spot. Monroe stopped them. "It's not about the money. Leave that shit here."

He took one last look at the destruction that he had caused before he walked out, leaving a pile of ash where Zyir's number one money spot used to be.

✳✳✳

"Yo' man Money is on some other shit," Fly Boogie stated as he lay in the hospital bed with a colonoscopy bag attached to his stomach. "The nigga might as well have killed me, bro! I can't get no pussy carrying around this fucking shit bag."

Zyir smirked at the young kid's sense of humor at a crucial time like this.

"The nigga burnt the shit to the ground like it was nothing. Had hoes screaming for they lives, ya feel me? I can still smell the bodies, fam. On some real shit, it was like Mecca's ghost flew into that nigga. The streets ain't seen a massacre like that since Mecca."

Zyir saw red as he listened to Fly Boogie tell his version of what had gone down. Monroe had taken their beef public by personally attacking The Cartel. Usually the one to strike first, Zyir kicked himself for hesitating. He had wanted to handle Monroe accordingly, seeing as how his demise would crush Breeze, but Money wasn't holding any punches. He was forcing Zyir's hand, and now they were on some gangster shit.

"You ready to put in some work? I need you on the team so I can see firsthand some of the stories I been hearing about you," Zyir said. "Your murder game proper?"

"No doubt, big homie, my shit's official. Only reason these niggas caught me slipping is because I thought my man was family. Won't happen again, I'll tell you that," Fly Boogie stated with venom lacing his tone.

"A'ight, rest up. You're gonna need it. And hold on to that for me," Zyir said as he slyly passed Fly Boogie a burner.

"Good looking, bro. I felt naked than a muuuu'fucka without my joint," Fly Boogie replied. "Holla at me though. Whatever you need done, I got it. I'm about that work."

Zyir nodded and then made his exit. The two goons he had posted outside the door followed him out as he headed to see Carter; all the while murder plots played in his head.

Chapter 16

"She's not to be underestimated."
—Monroe

"You niggas ready to make a name for yourselves, right?" Monroe asked as he sat at the table with three youngsters. He had recruited them from Opa-locka for a specific job and they all were hungry live wires. They were the type of goons who killed for nothing. They were looking for a come up, so when Monroe knocked on the door with an opportunity, they were ecstatic.

"No doubt. What we got to do?" the oldest of the young clique asked. Monroe smiled and rubbed his hands together, as he quickly scanned the nearly empty restaurant.

"I need a job done and I need it done right. I need a bitch kidnapped," Monroe said without blinking an eye.

"Kidnapped?" the kid asked as a smile formed on his face. "Shit's easy, son. We a'snatch that bitch up. Just point us to her. We will handle the rest, big homie," he said with confidence as the two other goons nodded in approval.

"Nah, li'l nigga. You are going about it all wrong. It's not an easy job. This isn't an ordinary chick. I mean . . . she move like a nigga. She is not to be underestimated, so I need this done right with no mishaps. You got me?"

"I got you. We just need the rundown on the bitch. You want us to slump her?" the goon asked as he began to lick his chops, eager to kill. He wanted to put in work so badly.

Monroe shook his head in frustration and folded his hands together, trying not to show his frustration. "Listen close. I want you to snatch her up. That's it! Understand?"

"Got it," the leader said.

"Meet me here tomorrow at the same time and I will give you all the info. I'm going to set up a spot that I want you to take her to. Once she's there, tie her up and wait for me. You do that and I got twenty-five stacks for you . . . apiece," Monroe stated.

"Apiece?" they all asked in unison, not believing what they had just heard. They would have done it for free, but to find out that they was about to get paid handsomely, it was a bonus.

"That's right. If you guys pull this off, I will put all of you on. No more small-time shit, li'l nigga. Welcome to the big leagues. You have the ticket to the money train right in front of you. What you gon' do?" Monroe asked as he sat back in his chair and looked at each one of them in the eyes.

"We gon' get that money," the leader said. Pandora's box had just been opened, and Monroe knew that there was no coming back on what he had just put in motion.

***

Miamor looked at the paper in her hands and smiled seeing her baby's ultrasound pictures. She couldn't wait to show Carter. The baby was getting so big, and the realization that she would finally be a mother hit her. This made her heart warm, and a smile spread across her face involuntarily. Just as the thought of

Carter danced in her mind, her phone rang. She looked at the caller ID and saw that is was him calling.

"Hey, baby. I was just—"

"Look, Mia. Listen very closely to me. I need you to check into a room in South Beach. Do not go home," Carter said, cutting her off midsentence. Miamor could sense the urgency in his voice, something very rare with Carter. He seemed worried.

"Wait, wait. What's wrong, baby? Is everything okay?" Miamor asked as the smile that was just on her face turned into a confused frown.

"Everything is okay. I just need you to do that for me. As soon as you get there and check in, text me the room number. I will meet you there later tonight," Carter instructed.

"Carter, you are scaring me. Tell me what is going on," she demanded as she made her way over to her car.

"Just do what I said and I will explain it to you later tonight, okay?" he responded.

"Okay. Carter . . . I love you," Miamor said as she stopped walking for a brief second.

"I love you too," Carter said just before he hung up the phone. Miamor pushed the end button on her phone and headed directly to her car. She began to get a bad feeling in the pit of her stomach and she hated the feeling. She knew something was wrong. She had never heard Carter sound so anxious.

Miamor hurried to her car and started it, looking around apprehensively. She pulled out of the parking lot and fixed her rearview mirror. She was growing nervous and paranoid because of Carter's instructions. She maneuvered through the streets and headed toward South Beach. "I don't know what's going on, Carter, but—" Her thoughts were interrupted by a bum walking across the street and she hit her brakes abruptly, stopping just short of him. Her whole body tensed up, and she blew her horn to alert him. Just as Miamor made eye contact with the bum, a black truck pulled up next to Miamor's car with three youngsters inside. Miamor held her breath as she noticed the menacing looks on their faces and knew that something wasn't right. All three pairs of eyes were on her, and she felt her heart begin to pound hard. She noticed that their eyes looked past her, and she followed their eyes. Before she could react, a black van pulled up on the opposite side and a masked man jumped out and got into her car. He had a gun to her head and threw her car in park.

"Nooo!" she yelled as everything happened so fast. The bum pointed a gun at the young boys as his partner grabbed up Miamor and forced her into the van. The youngsters were defenseless as they had their hands in the air. The goon posing as a bum walked backward to the van and hopped in. The sound of screeching tires filled the air as they bent the corner and sped off.

A black pillowcase was put over Miamor's head as she cried for Carter, but he couldn't hear her. No one could.

Chapter 17

"You either let me walk out of here or
Carter will send his goons to get me . . ."
—Miamor

Miamor coughed uncontrollably as she struggled to catch her breath. She had no idea how long she had been out, but as she opened her eyes she was hit with a splitting headache. Her mouth fell open in distress, but no sound came out as she grimaced in pain. *Where am I?* she thought.

Surprisingly, she was left unbound, and she hesitantly stood to her feet. Miamor's eyes danced around the room to find something to defend herself with as her heart raced. The room was small but comfortable. A queen bed and a bureau were the only contents of the room, but with no window Miamor was unsure of what time of day it was. Had she been out for hours or days? How long had she been gone? Did Carter realize she was missing? Miamor was at a mental loss as she tried to assess her current unfortunate event.

A greasy bag of food sat on top of the dresser, and Miamor silently went over to it, emptying the contents. A burger and fries sat inside. She bypassed the food and opened the drawers, hoping to find anything that she could use to protect herself. A gun would have been nice, but Miamor wasn't picky. A pen, a wire hanger . . . she'd take anything at this point, but to her dismay all of the drawers were empty. She had been tossed into an empty room, and her imagination was getting the best of her. The longer she waited, the more worry filled her heart.

Miamor had never been afraid of anything in her life, but as she sat waiting for the unknown, she feared for the life of her unborn child. Maternal instinct caused her to think of the seed growing in her belly before thinking of herself. *Where the fuck am I?* she thought uneasily.

Her frustration grew until she couldn't contain herself. Fuck waiting for someone to come; she was going to make them come. Miamor walked over to the door and kicked it as hard as she could.

BAM! BAM! BAM!

Always one to confront her attackers, she wanted to see who she was up against. She wasn't about to cower and have the hours of the day tick by torturously slow. Someone had wanted her; now she was here, and she wanted to know the who's and why's behind the setup.

"I know you're out there! Who are you? If you think someone isn't looking for me at this very moment you got the game fucked up! Do you know who I am?" she screamed as she beat the door with her fists, causing a commotion.

Miamor had been a part of the streets long enough to know that whoever had taken her wanted something. Otherwise she would be dead already. Her first thought told her that Monroe was behind it. He had more than enough reason to want her extinct, but something about the situation just didn't feel right. The new sheets on the bed, the mediocre but accommodating setup, the meal—none of it was Monroe's style. *Money would have put me in a dirt hole by now,* Miamor thought. At the least he would have gagged and bound her. The freedom of movement and speech was a luxury in this situation, and it was one that Monroe would not have afforded her.

Miamor lifted her foot to kick the door once more, but momentum caused her to stumble forward slightly as the door opened.

A masked goon entered the room, enraged at her outbursts. She was loud, screaming at the top of her lungs. They were in the middle of nowhere, in the Florida Everglades to be exact, and there was no one around to hear her, but he'd be damned if he listened to her wails all night. "Bitch, get your ass over there and shut the fuck up before I cut your tongue from your fucking throat!" he ordered as he grabbed her roughly and threw her onto the bed.

It took everything in Miamor not to come out of her mouth crazy at the dude in front of her. Fire danced in her eyes as she stared him down maliciously. Her pride told her to pop off, but the flutters of her child kicking in her stomach won the battle of reason, making her play it cool.

"I'm sorry. Please, I just want to go home. What do you want? Is it money? I have money. I can get you—"

"Shut the fuck up!" the goon yelled. A hard slap to her face caused Miamor to see stars, and she curled on the bed in a fetal position as she held her injured jaw.

The goon stared lustfully at Miamor. Her breasts heaved under the thin fabric of the Chanel dress she wore and her ass could barely be contained, while her hips caused the hemline to rise. She held her face as she squirmed across the bed, putting her back against the wall.

"Where you going? Huh? You running? I bet you run from the dick just like that, don't you?" the goon asked as he hovered over Miamor, grabbing at her legs. Miamor kicked his hands away as she panicked. Carter's face flashed through her mind. She needed him now more than ever.

"No!" she screamed as her foot met with his mouth.

"Fuck! You bitch!" the goon shouted in pain. Her protests only made him angrier, and despite the strict instructions he had been given regarding the job, he decided that he would have a piece of Miamor. She was too enticing not to sample. Her gripped her thighs with both hands and pulled her forcefully toward him. His hands squeezed her skin so tightly that he left bruises where each one of his fingertips dug into her flesh.

"Don't do this, please. I'm pregnant," she whispered as he climbed on top of her and pulled out his dick. A crooked leer spread across his face, and he lowered himself, positioning for entry.

"Even better," he cracked. "That's the best pussy."

Miamor wanted to fight him, but he was three times bigger than her. The only thing she could think of was something happening to her child. If he hit her hard enough, in just the right spot, it could endanger her seed, and she had to protect that at all costs. She was in a delicate state, and her body stiffened at the foreign touch of another man.

He opened her legs with such force that it felt as if her pelvis cracked. Tears flooded her vision. In the past he would have had to kill her to take what he wanted, but things were so different. Now, she had something to live for. Now, she would sacrifice a piece of her soul in order to survive. She lay stiff like a cadaver and closed her eyes as the goon ripped her panties. Her chest heaved in distress and . . .

BOOM!

The gunshot rang in her ears, forcing her eyes open as the weight of the goon collapsed over her. His now limp body pushed the wind from her lungs, and she placed her hands on his dead chest and rolled him off of her.

Her body shook as his blood covered her dress and she looked up into the eyes of his killer. He was masked, but there was something familiar about him. The dark eyes that looked through the holes in the ski mask penetrated her. He saw through her.

She squinted curiously as she opened her mouth to speak. "What do you want from me?" she asked.

"I just want you, little mama. That's it and nothing more," the masked man responded.

Her eyes widened in surprise as she rushed to stand. Her mouth opened slightly in disbelief. *This can't be happening. This isn't real. He wouldn't do this to me,* she thought. The gun that now hung at his side, gripped loosely in his hand, did nothing to stop Miamor from crossing the room. She reached up to remove his mask, but a firm hand gripped her wrist to stop her. They stood there for a moment, Miamor looking through the eyes of a killer as she shook her head.

"It's not you," she whispered. "Is it?" she added unsurely. The goon released her hand and Miamor pulled off his mask.

"Murder . . ." The whisper could barely be heard as she backpedaled away from him.

"I missed you, li'l mama," he replied.

Mixed emotions filled her. He had taught her everything she knew and was the first man she had ever loved.

"Murder?" she repeated in confusion, unable to wrap her mind around what was happening. Suddenly it was all so overwhelming. Rage bubbled to the top, over everything else. "Why would you do this to me?" she asked as she charged him, pushing him in the chest in frustration.

Murder took her assault as she released years of pent-up resentment. The question wasn't vague. It was deeper than just her kidnapping. When Murder had been sent away to prison, her entire world had changed.

"You've been out of my life for years! You just can't show up here! You can't just come back!" Her anger turned to sadness as the things she felt for him in the past came rushing back to her. He was the only person who had ever seen her softer side. He knew her before she was an infamous Murder Mama. He had groomed her.

Her resolve softened as she found comfort in his embrace, and she cried on his shoulder as his arms closed around her.

"It's all right," Murder whispered as he pulled her tightly to his chest, holding the back of her head securely, his fingers lost in her hair. "Let's get you cleaned up and let me take care of this nigga. After that we'll talk and I'll explain everything to you."

She pushed away from him, gathering her composure. "I don't want to hear an explanation, Murder. I want to go home," she said, her voice low. She couldn't look him in the eyes, because the sincerity she saw in them took her down memory lane. In the past her affection for him had been so strong that she couldn't deny him, but now things had changed. Now Carter had entered the picture, and her feelings for Murder dwindled when measured against her love for Carter.

"I am home, Miamor. I came all the way down here to bring you home. I took on the biggest drug organization just to get you back. When I thought you were dead, I hunted these niggas, Miamor. Somebody was going to pay for what I thought happened to you, but when you resurfaced, I had to have you. You crossed my mind every day while I was locked up. Your face kept me alive in there, and I'm not leaving Miami without you, li'l mama," he answered, his voice serious.

"So you kidnap me? You snatch me off the streets and put me in harm's way?" Miamor argued. His words tugged at her heart's strings, but angered her all the same.

"You were never in any danger," Murder said. "Just give me a minute to explain, Miamor. Get out of the bloody clothes and just come sit down and talk to me. This is me. You can't tell me that you're not happy to see me." Murder walked up on her and placed his hand beneath her chin. "You can't say you didn't miss me."

Miamor turned her head and attempted to walk around him, out of the room. He grabbed her arm and turned her back to him.

"You're not leaving. I'm sorry," he stated sternly.

Miamor scoffed in disbelief. "So you're going to force me to stay? You're keeping me here when I'm telling you I want to leave!"

Murder was visibly wounded by her words. "I'm asking you to give me a week. I know you, Miamor. The life you're living ain't you. You don't want to be wifey to a nigga like Carter. The nigga's pussy. All of this Cartel bullshit. You telling me that's the life you want? That ain't you. You're a loner. You're a recluse. The only family you love was the little one that we created. Me, you, and . . ."

"My sister," Miamor whispered as she closed her eyes and saw Anisa's face in her head.

"You laying up with the very niggas that took her life, Miamor! She in the dirt and you sitting on a throne with the mu'fuckas who murked her. That ain't you. You don't want that. I know you. That nigga Carter has got you brainwashed, li'l mama. Just give me a week to remind you of who you are," Murder bargained.

"I know who I am," Miamor replied. "I'm with Carter because I want to be. No brainwashing, no angles, I love him. Fuck a week. I'm not looking back to the past, Murder. You're the past, and I'm leaving all of that shit behind. Now you either let me walk out of here or Carter will send his goons to get me, but either way I'm leaving. He'll never stop looking for me, Murder, and you don't know what I know. His reach in the streets is long. He'll find me."

"It hasn't been that long, Miamor. You know how I get down. The nigga bring smoke to my doorstep and I'ma leave him leaking on it," Murder replied venomously. "Now go take a shower and clean yourself up. You try to run and I'll rip that baby right out of your stomach."

Miamor blinked away her tears. "And that's love? You came back here because you love me, right? Love don't do shit like that, Murder."

"I love every piece of you, but I hate every part of him, including . . ." His words trailed off as he pointed to her stomach.

Miamor knew him well enough to know that he wasn't lying. He didn't use scare tactics. If he said it, he meant it. *Carter, please come for me,* she thought. Miamor was superior to every nigga she had ever gone up against with the exception of Murder. He knew her too well for her to have the upper hand.

"How could you, Mia? You were my li'l mama," Murder asked. "Now you're pregnant with this nigga bastard kid."

Miamor broke down, hearing his heartbreak and feeling heartbreak of her own as she thought of her fate. It was possible that she wouldn't make it out of this one alive. She gave him no response besides the sobs that racked her.

"Get out of the bloody clothes. By the time you get out of the shower, I'll have dinner for you and I'll take care of this mess," he said, pointing to the goon's dead body. He kissed the top of her head, and she closed her eyes in despair as he exited the room.

Miamor was stuck between a rock and a hard place. She wanted to hate Murder, but she couldn't. She knew that he had been locked up for so long that she was all he remembered. His world had been on a standstill while hers had moved on. There was a time when she thought that she would never replace him, but upon meeting Carter, all of her doubts had gone out of the window. He was the greatest man she had ever known, and her loyalty was with him. Miamor just had to figure out how to get back to him in one piece.

✳✳✳

By the time Miamor emerged from the bathroom, the dead body was gone and Murder stood outside the bathroom door, waiting patiently for her. He held a shopping bag for her.

"It's not designer like what you're used to, but it'll do," he said.

Miamor held the cotton towel tightly around her body and took the bag from Murder. Murder tugged at the towel that was tucked snugly under her armpits.

"Murder . . . don't," she said.

He snatched the towel anyway and pulled it away from her, revealing her naked body. "Relax, li'l mama. I never had to take it," Murder said.

His hands explored her body as he slowly ran his hands over her stomach. She was perfectly sculpted, but her once flawless body was marred with scars. They showed the struggles she had endured at the hands of Mecca Diamond. Her baby bump was subtle and barely there, but Murder knew her so well that he knew that she was pregnant without her having to tell him. He noticed the slight weight in her face and the thickness around her hips and breasts.

Miamor's breath caught in her throat as she waited for him to hurt her, to hit her in the stomach and hurt her unborn child. She was surprised when she felt how gently he touched her. His hands graced her like feathers, and she placed her hands over his.

"This is supposed to be us, li'l mama. This is supposed to be us . . . our baby," Murder said. Miamor removed his hand, squirming out of his grasp as she covered herself with the towel.

"Things have changed, Murder. I've changed. A part of me will always care about you, but I love Carter. Since you're not leaving me any choice, I'll stay a week, but I don't want to mislead you. I will not stay after that. If you try to make me, you will have to sleep with one eye open for as long as I'm here, because the first opportunity I get, I'll kill you," she said.

Murder pushed her against the wall, trapping her in his personal space as his hand went to her neck. Miamor tensed. "You couldn't kill me any quicker than I could kill you," Murder said. His hand moved from her neck to her cheek as he traced her jaw line. "I'd always hesitate, and we both know that in the murder game there is no room for second-guessing. Thank you for the week, though. By the end of it, you won't want to go home."

Chapter 18

"I want anybody affiliated with them to be in
pieces in the Atlantic. Fish food."
—Carter

Carter paced back and forth with worry on his mind,
but his heart was ablaze with anger. Zyir had as-
sembled the entire Cartel at Carter's request. They all
sat silently. No one dared to say a word as they waited
uneasily for Carter to speak first. Everyone seated at
the table knew that there were two people in Carter's
life who were off-limits—Miamor and Breeze. Someone
had disrespected him, and the veins bulging out of his
neck indicated that someone's life was on an official
countdown. He held his hands behind his back as he
his jaw tensed.

Zyir stood ominously in the background, rubbing his
chin as he bowed his head while leaning against the
wall. He was the leader of The Cartel. Unlike Monroe,
Zyir wasn't threatened by a brotherhood of power. Zyir
was the face that the streets saw. Carter had put him in
the forefront of The Cartel, and he wore his crown with
humility. If Carter wanted to step back into his seat,
Zyir would step aside and support his decision. It was
love and loyalty that kept Zyir and Carter on the same
page. There was no competition between them because
there were no weak links in their chain. They reigned
over Miami as a team. Monroe wanted it all for himself,

and in his attempts to overthrow The Cartel, he had crossed the line.

Carter had been feeling extreme guilt in his decision to press the button on Monroe, but now that Miamor had been snatched, Carter felt no remorse. All bets were off and nothing was off limits. If Monroe wanted to play hardball, then Carter would school him on the rules of the game. Monroe had put down a play that couldn't be taken back, and now Carter was all in. This was different than the war with the Haitians. This was more serious than the beef with the Mexican cartels. This was blood against blood, and the aftermath of their war would be one that could level everything that The Cartel had built over the years.

Carter was strategic in the way he chose his words as he addressed the heads of his empire.

"Something has been taken from me. Someone dear to me has been touched. A line has been crossed. I've got a hundred racks for whoever can bring Monroe Diamond to me. I don't want him harmed, just delivered to me. I've got ten thousand dollars for any members of O.M.G. I want anybody affiliated with them to be in pieces in the Atlantic. Fish food," Carter stated, his voice even, like the calm before the storm.

Zyir could see the anger simmering in Carter's heart, and he recognized the thirsty look in the eyes of the hustlers who sat around the table. Carter had put a six-figure bounty out on the streets, and niggas were determined to make that cake.

Carter dismissed the room, and Zyir stayed back as the rest of the men exited the house. Tension was high, and Zyir didn't know what to say to reassure Carter. They had been through thick times before and had weathered the storm, but the current opposition was someone who occupied space inside Carter's heart. There was no easy answer, no easy out. Whatever he decided would destroy him, the same way that killing Mecca had. He was about to annihilate another brother on behalf of the woman he loved.

"She's pregnant, fam. She's carrying my kid and a nigga got her tied up somewhere," Carter stated in disbelief. If she hadn't been expecting, Carter would have more confidence that Miamor could hold things down. She wasn't the average victim, and vulnerability wasn't a characteristic that she showed often, but in her current state there was no way that she could defend herself. Carter had to get her back home. If something happened to her, Carter would never forgive himself. She was his woman. She was his responsibility, and the baby growing in her stomach meant everything to him. Carter felt as if his worst fear was coming true. He had promised Miamor that he would take care of her if she laid down her gun, and now that she had, he had failed her.

"If something happens to her or my baby, I'm going to paint the fucking city red," Carter said as he walked over to the picture window that looked out over his beautifully landscaped estate.

"It won't. I'll put my ear to the streets. Somebody knows something. If I hear anything I'll hit you, fam," Zyir said. He gave Carter a reassuring pat on the back before making his exit.

***

Carter sat in his black Porsche Cayenne, maneuvering through the streets on black rims and hidden behind the black tint as he headed to Coral Gables. He knew where he could find Monroe. Just months ago it was he who had helped his younger brother pick out the secluded estate. He rode in silence, his heart clenched like an iron fist inside his chest, and his stomach felt hollow.

Since Miamor's return he had held out on her, not wanting to give her his all just in case she betrayed him again. Now he realized that no matter how hard he tried to keep his feelings for her at bay, she had him. Miamor captured his soul and his heart in her hands, and without her he felt empty. He would kill a nigga for her, including his brother. There was no exception when it came to her. Now that she was pregnant with his son, he would never allow anyone to bring harm to them.

As he drove, the city gradually disappeared and he turned right onto the uncharted road that led to Monroe's estate.

Since establishing O.M.G., Monroe lived like something out of the movies. A guard sat in the security booth outside the gated home, and three more patrolled the perimeter of the grounds. There were cameras everywhere, and two beautiful black Rottweiler pups made the plush estate seem more like a prison than a place one called home. Monroe had taken all of these measures to ensure that Carter could not touch him, but he had forgotten one thing. Carter was the one who had set him up with the security company in the first place. After a hefty $25,000 payment, Carter had easily purchased the code to Monroe's gate and the blind eye of the security guards on payroll. Carter nodded to the guard at the gate as he keyed in the access code.

The electronic black steel gate swung open and Carter guided his car inside. He pulled directly to the front of the home, parking his car in the circular driveway. Taking a deep breath, he pressed a button on his console and watched the hidden compartment slide out. It was a trick he had put Zyir up on and a necessity for every car that he owned.

He removed his Glock .40 handgun and kept it in his hand as he got out, approaching the door. Two ferocious dogs came running toward him, barking their threats. They were two beauties, a black man's stallion, but Carter didn't hesitate to lay them down. He shot them down at his feet, delivering one bullet each before stepping over their bodies and knocking on Monroe's door.

The butt of the gun caused his knocks to sound like thunder as he beat down the door. He didn't want his visit to be a surprise. He was there to confront Monroe head on and negotiate Miamor's release. He wasn't leaving without her, and he hoped for Monroe's sake that he made this simple, because Carter was prepared to make things difficult.

The door flew open, and Carter was surprised to see Leena standing on the other side of the door. She stood clinging to her silk robe, her hair slightly messy, as she looked at Carter in confusion. Clearly she hadn't been expecting anyone. Her presence had slipped his mind, but it definitely sweetened the pot.

"Carter!" she exclaimed in surprise.

"Where is Money?" he asked. His voice froze her instantly as her eyes shifted to the gun in his hand and her brow wrinkled in worry.

"He's not here," she replied. "Should I be afraid to let you in here right now, Carter? Your nephew is in here." She closed the door a bit and spoke to him through a small opening as she tried to keep him on the outside of her home. He had always been gracious to her. He was family, but the murderous look in his eyes and the fact that he stood at her door, gun in hand, caused her much distress.

Carter eased her inside the house, using his weight to push her aside, and then closed the door behind him.

"I'm sorry, Leena. Money took something from me; now I have to take something from him."

✳✳✳

"Leena!" Monroe screamed as he stormed into his home. He recognized Carter's car as soon as he pulled up, and the dead dogs out front prepared him for the worst. "Leena!"

"No need to yell, Money. She's still alive . . . for now," Carter said, his voice low and threatening as he watched Monroe enter the living room. Leena held her sleeping son in her arms as tears of fear fell down her cheeks while sitting in a chair at Carter's gunpoint.

"Money, please," she sobbed as Carter held the gun at point-blank range, preparing to blow her brains out.

"What are you doing? My fucking family, Carter! This is how you want to play it?" Money barked.

"Why not, little brother? This is how you're playing it. My girl and my seed are missing. She's carrying your nephew, Money. My son! This is out of character for me, but please don't doubt that I will take everything from you right now with just the pull of a trigger. You give me back my family and I'll leave your home without harming yours. Where is she?" Carter asked with murderous intent in his eyes. His heart galloped with adrenaline as his temper flared.

Carter wanted to put a hollow point between Monroe's eyes. For Monroe to have the audacity to snatch Miamor was a show of disrespect. Had he been any other nigga, Monroe would already be mourning the loss of his bitch and kid, but because they shared the same blood, Carter was throwing him a line of redemption. One chance was all Monroe had to right his wrong.

"Carter, I don't know what the fuck you're talking about. We're at odds, but I would never—"

"Never torch my stash houses, never shoot up my blocks? What are your limits, Money? Miamor is missing! You're the only nigga in the city that has the balls to come at me like that. You put in the call to them O.M.G. niggas and have her released now," Carter demanded.

"Carter, I swear to God, fam—"

"Money, I've been going easy on you because you're my brother, and you have obviously mistaken my kindness for weakness. You've got five seconds before you're planning a double funeral," Carter threatened.

Leena broke down as she cradled her son to her chest. His tiny hands clung to her as she closed her eyes and prayed over him. She cringed as the cold steel marked the kiss of death on the back of her skull. "I will put her brains on the floor!" Carter yelled.

"Carter!" Money yelled in distress as he watched his family squirm as his son awoke from the commotion and began to reach for him. Leena held on to their child tightly, however, as she was racked with heartbreak.

"Money, just tell him what he wants to know," Leena begged. "Please."

"Five," Carter began his countdown, eyes cold and his will unflinching.

"Don't. You don't want to do this," Money negotiated. His hands were extended as if he could calm Carter. He wanted to shoot him dead where he stood, but he would never make such a risky move as long as his love and child were in harm's way.

"Four," Carter continued.

"I don't have her, Carter," Money said.

"Three . . . Where is she, Money?" Carter demanded.

Money's eyes widened. "Carter!"

"Two!" Carter moved the gun from Leena to Monroe Jr.

"He's my son!" Money protested, anxiety causing his voice to raise an octave as his eyes grew as wide as saucers.

"One."

Monroe dropped to his knees and extended both hands in a desperate plea as tears blurred his vision. "I don't have her!" Money yelled. "It wasn't me! That wasn't my play! I didn't take Miamor! I admit I thought about it! I had my people in place, but someone else got there first!"

Carter fingered the trigger.

"No! Brother! I swear on everything it wasn't me. My little niggas were all set to go when somebody pulled up in black SUVs and did the job for us," Monroe said, the words spilling out of his mouth as sweat shone on his forehead.

"Who?" Carter barked.

"I don't know! All I know is that it wasn't me! Now please let your nephew and Leena go!"

Carter heard the sincerity in his words and he withdrew his gun. He knew that Monroe would never gamble with the lives of those he loved, especially the son he was just getting to know. *He's not behind this,* Carter thought as a new confusion swept over him. He had no other enemies. Who would make such a bold move against him?

Carter stepped away from a sobbing Leena and walked up to Monroe, who now stood on his feet. They stood toe to toe as they stared each other in the eyes.

"If you're lying, Money . . ."

"I'm not," Monroe responded. "Now get the fuck out of my house."

Monroe rushed over to his family as Carter stormed out.

***

Carter sat with the newspaper in front of him, staring at the dead faces of Monroe's security guards and the owner of the security company that employed them. Carter knew that Monroe had executed them for not protecting his home. The moment Carter stepped foot on his soil, the guards' lives had been put on a count-down. Carter didn't flinch or feel a sliver of remorse. As long as Miamor was missing, he didn't care how many people lost their lives in his persistent search to find her.

His bell rang, and one of his goons stood, instinctively placing a hand near his waist. Carter checked one of several monitors that were positioned discreetly around his mansion.

"Let her in," he said as he recognized Leena's face.

He stood and awaited her presence as she was given access to his mansion. She was the vision of beauty standing before him. Her flower-printed Prada dress flowed serenely behind her as she walked toward him while her heels clicked the floor. She stood across the room, twiddling her hands in front of her with worry written all over her face.

"I'm sorry it didn't work, Carter. I tried to make it look as real as possible, but your bastard brother would rather hold his secrets than to tell the truth to save me and his son," Leena said, her eyes watering. Carter would never put her or his nephew in harm's way. The clip wasn't even in the gun the night before when he held her at gunpoint to get Money's cooperation. "In one sentence he says he loves us, but when faced with a chance to prove it . . ."

"He loves you, Leena," Carter interrupted. "He wasn't lying. He doesn't have Miamor," Carter said. "This I'm sure of."

His words silenced her, and she looked down unsurely. "How can you be so sure?"

"I know my brother," Carter answered solemnly.

Leena had been around Carter long enough to see that he was hurting. His spirit was broken, and she could see the emotions taking a toll on him.

"She will be all right," Leena said, only half believing her words.

"Will she?" Carter replied.

Leena reached up and hugged Carter, planting a sisterly kiss on his cheek. "I have to get back. I'm not even supposed to be here. I told Monroe that I wouldn't leave the house, and the baby is with the nanny. I wish this war between you and your brother would end. I miss my family."

Carter kissed her forehead but didn't respond as he turned and walked out of the room.

Chapter 19

"What's a ring without a wedding?"
—Leena

Leena walked softly on the plush carpet as she approached Monroe's office. His door was wide open, and she stood there watching him nervously as she wrung her fingers in front of her body. He was intent, focused, powerful, and the most beautiful specimen of a man she had ever seen. Her heart thumped and she was overwhelmed with admiration every time she stood before him. He looked down at the paperwork before him, but was always aware of those around him. He sensed her presence the moment she had crept up.

"Come in here, beautiful," he said as he looked up from his busy work and sat back in his plush leather executive chair.

Leena walked in and rounded his desk until she stood directly between his legs.

"What's on your mind?" he asked her.

"That's what I've been wondering about you," she replied.

"Don't mince words, Lee. Tell me what's wrong, baby," he said.

"I miss Breeze and Carter and Zyir. Money, they're our family and this beef, this war, it's eating me up. It's not supposed to be like this," Leena said as she touched Monroe's face gently, making sure that he was looking her in the eyes. She needed him to feel the sincerity in her words. "Monroe misses his uncles, baby. They're all he knows."

Money's jaw tensed, but his temper didn't flare. Leena was his everything. He wished that his comeback could have been one big family reunion. He remembered the days of peace and unity within the Diamond clan, but it seemed that those times had died right along with his father, Carter Diamond. Maybe if Monroe had never gone away, then he could accept Zyir as family. He would have been around to see the love and loyalty that Zyir had proven time and time again. But as it stood, Monroe felt that Zyir was trying to take his place.

Monroe refused to feel like an outsider in his own organization, so he had built his own. The Opa-locka Money Gang showed him all the loyalty that a king deserved. The streets were eating his product up and no one, not even Zyir with all of his Cartel affiliation, could compete. If you weren't seated at Monroe's table then you didn't eat. He wasn't saving any sea bass for niggas who didn't rock with O.M.G.

"I need you to be like a chameleon, Leena. You have to be able to adapt to your surroundings. There are no guarantees in this lifestyle, Lee. The only thing that I can promise is that I will love you. I will love you until my body hits the dirt, and I will provide for you. You will be safe and we'll live life as long as God and the law lets me. The faces that surround us may change, and I need you to get used to that. Don't get too attached to anyone, because at any moment disloyalty can make them replaceable." Money pointed to his chest and then pointed to hers. "This is our family. You, me, and our son . . . we're all we got, and that's all you need." He lifted her left finger and admired the flawless stone that he had placed on it. "That's why I gave you this."

"What's a ring without a wedding?" she asked sadly. "With everything that's going on, when will we have time to get married?"

"We'll make time, Lee. We can do it whenever you want. In fact, planning a wedding will keep you occupied. We can do it tomorrow if you want," Monroe said with a charming smile.

Leena smiled. "I need a little more time than that," she answered wistfully as she began to daydream about colors and floral arrangements.

"There's my girl," Monroe said with a wink.

"How about a month. I can get with a wedding planner and it can be small and intimate. Maybe I can invite Breeze?" Leena said.

Monroe missed his sister, but in his attempt to keep the beef hidden from her, he had barely seen or reached out. She was a sensitive subject, and Leena could see the wheels in his head turning as he considered the possibility.

"How about two weeks?" he suggested as he kissed her nose.

Leena leaned back and wrinkled her brow. "What's the rush? What aren't you telling me?" she asked. It was unlike Monroe to jump so quickly into commitment, and she knew that there had to be an ulterior motive behind this sudden rush to matrimony.

"I want you to be my wife, Leena. I want you and my son to be secure. We're at war, and if something happens to me, I need to know that you're entitled to everything I have," Monroe said honestly. "It's important that I leave you with the world at your feet."

"Seems like we're planning your funeral, Money . . . not our wedding," she whispered. Leena rose from his lap and walked toward the door.

Monroe didn't want to hurt her feelings or diminish
her excitement, but he didn't want to lie to her. She
could have the romantic side of things. His love for her
was very real, but he knew that with street fame came
the possibility of death. He just wanted her to be prepared for it, and as his wife, she would be.

✳✳✳

Dear Carter,

I'm writing you this letter to let you know that I'm
safe. I staged an entire kidnapping to run away
from you. It was all fake. I didn't know how to tell
you that I wanted out, and the entire setup just
went too far. I hear that you're looking for me, that
you've killed trying to find me. I want you to stop. I
chose to leave you, Carter. No one forced me to. I
walked away. I was suffocating in your world, and
I can't go through life pretending that I am someone I'm not. I'm never coming back to you. Having
your child would have been the biggest mistake
I've ever made. I got an abortion, Carter. We're
too different, and at the end of the day you're my
enemy and your people took my sister from me.
I've disappeared before, but this time I promise I
won't return. Move on, because I have. We're just
not meant to be.

Miamor

The words on the paper knocked Carter off of his
feet, and he slowly sat down on his couch and lowered
his head. *I trusted you,* he thought as he felt his heart
splitting painfully in half. The earth felt as if it had

stopped spinning. He loosened his Gucci slim tie as if it would help him breathe, but he was still stifled. He couldn't inhale. Miamor had just pulled the rug from beneath him, and he was falling into an emotional black hole. She had done it once before, and now he kicked himself for even giving her a second chance. He had supplied her with the hope to better herself, but instead she had slipped a noose around his neck and sent him flying off of a chair.

"Magdalena!" he called as he stood to his feet.

"Yes, Mr. Jones," his housekeeper replied as she instantly appeared in front of him. The middle-aged woman stood before him in a maid's uniform, awaiting his request.

"Please box up all of Miamor's things. Place them in storage. She won't be coming back," Carter instructed. The housekeeper frowned yet nodded in compliance.

"And the baby's things? Would you like for me to box his belongings as well?" she asked.

It was at the mention of his seed that Carter's resolve weakened. His eyes burned, but he willed his devastation away as he replied, "No, leave the nursery exactly as it is."

He knew that there was no more baby to plan for, but he didn't have the strength to see the room return to a blank canvas with white walls.

Magdalena looked at him with sympathy.

"I'm sorry, Mr. Jones," she said. She didn't know the full story, but she could see the sadness hanging from Carter's shoulders like coats from a rack.

"Me too," he replied. He looked at the picture of Miamor that sat in a small frame on the mantle of his fireplace. He thought of the things that he had done for her, the people he had crossed for her, and wars that had started over her. It seemed as if he was always the one sacrificing to make them work, and still she was disloyal. He pulled the picture down and tossed it into the fire. "Me too."

✳✳✳

As the days passed Miamor grew resentful. She didn't want to be with Murder. She didn't need him in her life. His season had passed a long time ago, and he refused to accept the fact that she had moved on. His attempts at conversation were blocked by her obvious disdain for him, but he was patient. He looked at Miamor like a drug addict. She had become dependent on Carter, and he was determined to be her morphine. He was weaning her off. After the letter he had forged to him on her behalf, Carter would no longer be looking for her anyway. Little did Miamor know Murder had destroyed their bond with one little Dear John.

"You can't just keep me here," she said, her arms crossed as she sat across the room from him. "I'm pregnant. I need medical care. I need vitamins and checkups. I'm extremely high risk. I need to be home. Carter—"

Murder was on her in a flash, across the room, and flipping over the coffee table, clearing his path to get to her. "Don't mention the nigga name in my presence. You lucky I'm even letting you keep that fucking baby. I'm trying real hard to keep shit cool with you, Miamor. But you're pushing me! Shut the fuck up about that nigga. You're here until I say it's time to go. You're never going back to that nigga. When you stop being fucking stubborn you'll realize that's what's best for you."

"What happened to you in there? I don't even recognize you," Miamor said with tears in her eyes. "Since when do you treat me like this? Since when do you talk to me like this?"

"Since you started fucking the next nigga," Murder spat. "When you act like the old you, I'll become the old me."

Miamor shook her head, disgusted. It didn't matter what Murder did. He couldn't turn back the hands of time. She had outgrown him, plain and simple. "If I meant as much as you say I do, then you'd get me to a doctor. . . . You would let me go."

Chapter 20

"One to the heart. No head shots, no torture."
—Carter

"You're beautiful," Breeze said as she stood back and watched Leena try on the beautiful ivory wedding gown. It was Vera Wang, and although the popular wedding designer was booked clear through the next two seasons, Money had given her a bottomless budget to make his bride-to-be's dreams come true. Leena spun around and rushed to Breeze.

"You made it!" she squealed in joy as the two women embraced. "It's so good to see you!" Leena was genuinely elated to be around Breeze. The two women were more than close, and it had been too long since they last spoke.

"Of course I made it!" Breeze said. "You're getting married tomorrow, and I'm honored that you want me to be the first person to see the dress. It's amazing!"

Breeze noticed the sad look in Leena's eyes. "What's wrong? Why aren't you happy? This is what you want, right?"

Leena shook off her poor mood and masked it with an insincere smile. "Yes, I'm fine. Sorry. I guess I'm just nervous."

Breeze wasn't buying Leena's excuse, however. She frowned and turned to the saleswoman. "Could you excuse us for a moment?" Breeze asked. The woman exited the fitting room and Breeze grabbed Leena's hand. "This is not the face of a woman getting married tomorrow. Now spill."

"Things are complicated, Breeze. I love Money and he's good to me, but this isn't how I envisioned this day. It all feels a little rushed. You're not even in the wedding."

"Yeah, well, considering you decided this two weeks ago, I'd say that it is rushed," Breezed answered with a smile. "It doesn't matter, Leena. You are meant for Money and he is meant for you. As long as the two of you are happy, no one else matters. Besides, I'll be there. I wouldn't miss this day for the world."

"Does Zyir know you're here?" Leena asked.

"You asked me not to tell him so I didn't. He's been distant lately, focused on other things," Breeze said, more to herself than to Leena.

Leena knew that Breeze didn't know what was going on between Zyir and Monroe. As much as she wanted to tell her, it wasn't her place. Breeze was the baby of the family, and she had been through a lot. No one liked to add burdens to her delicate shoulders.

"But we're not talking about me, we're talking about you." Breeze turned Leena toward the mirror and stood behind her as they looked at the reflection. "Now where's the veil?" Breeze asked. She spotted it in a box on the floor and pulled it out, admiring it briefly before clipping it in Leena's hair.

They both gasped in amazement.

"Now that's the smile of a bride," Breeze said. "You're perfection."

They embraced and Breeze checked her Burberry wrist piece. "I've got to go, but I'll see you tomorrow. You're staying at Turnberry Isle tonight?" she asked.

"Yeah, Money put me in a suite there. The entire glam squad is coming in the morning," Leena said.

"I'll see you then, bright and early. I love you, Lee!" Breeze said as she headed for the door.

"Love you too! Don't be late!"

✳✳✳

Breeze leaned back against Zyir's chest as he held the book they were reading in front of him. It was a ritual that they had started when they first met, and to this very day they still read to one another every night that they were together.

"Flip the page, B," Zyir said.

Breeze sighed and turned it to the next page, but Zyir could tell that she had stopped indulging in the juicy exploits of *Six and Free* long ago. He put down the book and she didn't even protest. She was too distracted to notice.

"You want to be with Leena right now, don't you?" he whispered.

Breeze turned toward him in shock. It was as if he had read her mind.

"This is the first lie you've ever told me, baby girl, and I must say you're not very good at it," Zyir said. "I've known about the wedding since you found out. You're very loud on the phone, ma. Where'd you learn to whisper, a helicopter?"

Breeze laughed and cut her eyes as she exclaimed, "Why didn't you say something? I've been trying to keep this a secret for two weeks!" Breeze exhaled, relieved that the secret was out. She hit him playfully with the book they had been reading. "I know you think that I'm naïve, but just because I follow your lead, Zyir, doesn't mean I'm blind to the things happening around me."

"Why aren't you invited to the wedding? Why isn't Carter? Why haven't I talked to Money since that dinner at Carter's house?" Breeze asked. "I have a feeling; I'm just hoping that it's wrong. I don't want to have to choose between the men in my life."

Zyir kissed the top of her head and inhaled her angelic scent. Her Cashmere Mist perfume, her signature scent, enveloped him.

"Things have been . . ." He paused to choose his words carefully. He didn't want Breeze to know too much. How could he tell her that the first chance he got he was going to blow her brother's head off his shoulders? Admitting such would be marital suicide. It would destroy their relationship forever.

"Things have been what?" Breeze asked.

"Tense," he finished. "We're all trying to figure out our place in The Cartel." Before she could ask any more questions he added, "But that shouldn't stop you from being with Leena and your nephew tonight. I'll call a car for you."

"Promise me that you'll work things out with Money," she said.

"I can promise to try," Zyir replied honestly. She turned and kissed his lips.

"I need you to try your hardest, Zyir. He's my brother." Her eyes told him that a storm would come if anything happened to Monroe; little did she know that Monroe had signed his own death certificate. He would fall, and soon Breeze would have to decide exactly where she stood. Zyir only hoped that their love would be strong enough to endure.

He sent her with a driver to Leena's suite and watched her drive away. As soon as the taillights could no longer be seen, he called Carter.

"Zyir, is everything smooth, fam? It's late," Carter answered, seeing Zyir's name on his caller ID.

"The nigga Money is getting married tomorrow. This is the first time I've been able to pinpoint this nigga's location. I'm not invited, but I'ma be there, nah mean?" Zyir said.

Carter was silent as he weighed the pros and cons in his head. "I don't know, Zy. Shit could get messy. Leena and my nephew will be there," Carter said. He was still trying to figure out a way to keep the peace and restore balance to the situation, but Monroe was making it very difficult.

"I sent Breeze to Leena's suite in Aventura. Li'l man is there with them. My driver will be on call in the morning to take them to the wedding, only I've already made sure that they never get there. By the time they realize something's wrong, the nigga Money will be leaking at the altar," Zyir stated.

A lump formed in Carter's throat, but he fought his conscience and said, "Make it quick, Zy. One to the heart. No head shots, no torture."

His voice was sad, and he felt nothing but regret as he gave the nod of approval.

"We got to get him before he gets us," Zyir said. "He sent bullets flying through your windows, fam. If the shoe was on the other foot and he had a clear shot, Money would pull the trigger."

"I know," Carter answered. "What kind of brotherhood is this?" he asked. He sighed and finished, "Take care of it. That solves our beef problem, but we still need a new connect. I'll hop on a flight in the A.M. to the West Coast. I've got a few connections out there that might be able to accommodate us."

"Sounds good, fam. I'll hit you after that thing is taken care of," Zyir said. Zyir hung up the phone and a crooked smile crossed his handsome, youthful face. Carter had just given him the green light, and it was all the permission he needed to make Monroe Diamond extinct.

Chapter 21

"I want shrimp and lobster, naked bitches and good pussy, linen suits and ocean views."
—Polo

Carter looked out into the night sky from the window of his private jet. In deep contemplation, he couldn't help but to think of Miamor. He shook his head, tossing her from his train of thought, and focused on the task at hand. He sank deeper into the plush leather seats.

He was bound for sunny California—Los Angeles to be exact, where he hoped to link up with his father's old running partner, Polo. The streets were a perfect distraction from Miamor, and he was ready to jump back in headfirst.

Monroe only had the game locked because Carter had allowed him room to eat. With his shark Zyir on his tail, it was only a matter of time before Monroe was out of the picture. His reign would be short-lived indeed, but it was a choice that Monroe had made the moment he had turned against the family. Carter knew that Monroe's death was one that would tear his entire family apart, but also a death that was necessary. His heart could not be any more broken than it was so fuck it, he was sending the Grim Reaper to Monroe's door with no remorse.

The pilot prepared for landing, and Carter gazed out over the lights of the city. Polo wasn't expecting him. Carter never liked to let anyone know his next move; the unexpected was always the safest way to move. That way no one could see him coming. In fact, Polo thought he was living in seclusion, cut off from all of his Miami ties. Little did he know that Carter had always known where he was, down to the four numbers on his mailbox.

As the plane made its final descent over the city, Carter gathered himself. Polo would definitely know where to go to get the product that Carter needed, and he wanted to hit the ground running. This wasn't a parlay trip. It was all business all the time for Carter, and he wasn't leaving without a brand-new cocaine connect. He wouldn't complain if he could corner the heroin trade either. Prescription drugs even. Los Angeles was the land of opportunity, and Carter was going to take advantage of the things it had to offer.

A black Maybach waited at the end of the clear port upon Carter's arrival, and he wasted no time instructing the driver how to get to Polo's Santa Monica apartment. He wondered why someone who had hustled so large now lived so small, and he vowed to make smart money moves with his dough so that he wouldn't end up living mediocre after his own retirement.

As the driver pulled onto Polo's street, Carter sat up attentively as he surveyed the area. "Spin the block for me," Carter instructed the driver, who nodded in reply. His paranoia was what kept him free and living. Many niggas had gotten caught slipping by being too relaxed. Carter would rather be safe than sorry. "Park up front. Do not move the car under any circumstances," Carter said.

"Yes, sir," the driver responded. He got out of the car and opened Carter's door.

Carter emerged and buttoned his Ferragamo suit jacket before heading to the entrance. The building was nice, luxurious even, and sat across the street from the Santa Monica beach, but still Carter wondered why Polo wasn't put up in a Beverly Hills estate. Ownership was key in Carter's book. Why lease a unit when you can own the building?

He knocked at Polo's door. It had been half a decade since they had last seen one another. He hoped his father's right-hand man was well, and he was eager to check in on him. The door opened, and Carter stood face to face with Polo the God a.k.a Uncle Polo, the godfather to all of Carter Diamond's children, including Carter Jones. Recognition registered in his gaze, but the words that came out of his mouth didn't match.

"Who are you?" he asked.

Carter stepped back, thrown off guard as he frowned. "It's me, Carter," he replied in confusion. "You don't know who I am?"

Polo shooed him away from his door. "G'on, young'un. Ain't nothing for you at my door. It's a young lady live a few doors down. You got the wrong apartment number, son," he said.

Before Carter could get another word out, the door was slammed in his face. Carter stood there for a second, stunned and obviously lost. He turned around and walked hesitantly away from the door. He looked back at the closed door, wondering what the hell that was all about. *I'll come back tomorrow,* he thought, hoping that Polo hadn't gone crazy from baking in the hot L.A. sun.

Carter checked into one of the swankiest five-star hotels in West Hollywood, reserving the penthouse suite for his stay. After tipping the bellman to deliver his bags, he was escorted by the concierge to the fiftieth floor.

Italian marble graced the floor, and the expansive floor-to-ceiling windows made Carter feel as if he were the king of the city. All of L.A. was at his feet as he looked out over the nightlife. The concierge left him well appointed with his requested vintage bottle of wine and a steak dinner already prepared and waiting for him to enjoy. He tipped the man generously and then sat down at the large dining table to indulge in his dinner for one.

He looked at the vacant chair across from him and emptiness filled his chest. His thoughts drifted to Miamor. Her absence was suffocating Carter, and he had never felt more alone than he did in that moment. He should be courting her all over the city, wining and dining, shopping and sightseeing. Instead he was solo and missing life as it passed him by.

BUZZ!

The bell to the room rang, and Carter stood, knowing that it was his bags being delivered. He grabbed a twenty dollar bill out of his money clip and headed for the door. He pulled it open.

"Young Carter."

"Hello, Polo," Carter replied as he embraced him. "It's good to see you. I thought you had lost your wit for a minute there, old man. What was that all about?" Carter asked in confusion.

Polo pointed to the steak that could be smelled clear across the room. "Why don't you order another one of those three hundred dollar steak dinners and let me fill you in?"

The two men sat over dinner, and Polo cut into his steak. He savored the flavor and said, "Now that's a steak."

Carter chuckled. "How did you know where I was staying?"

"You're Carter Diamond's son. I picked the most expensive hotel in L.A.," Polo said. "But look, you can't just show up out here unannounced. I've got a lot going on out here—things that you don't want to get wrapped up in."

"Try me," Carter said, fishing for more details.

"What I'm about to tell you will probably make me look like a snake, but it's the only thing keeping me free. After I left Miami, I began cooperating with the Feds against Estes," Polo admitted.

Carter put down his knife and fork, and his eyes immediately went to the door.

"You don't have to worry about them, Carter. They didn't follow me here, but they are watching every single person that steps foot to my door. That's why when you showed up out of the blue I acted like I'd never seen you before," Polo explained. "The last thing you need are ties to me. That'll automatically put you under a federal scope."

Carter silently kicked himself for walking right into the middle of a federal investigation. He knew that the DEA was the most thorough crime fighter on the planet. They had a war against drugs that had taken down some of the greats in the game. Just by putting his face on their cameras he knew that they would be asking who he was and what he did. He had drawn attention to himself.

"Are you wired?" Carter asked sternly.

"What? No, never against you," Polo assured.

Carter pulled his pistol off of his hip and placed it on the table. "Then you won't have a problem standing and unbuttoning your shirt," Carter said.

Polo paused briefly, slightly offended that Carter wanted proof, but as a major player in the game, he understood. He stood and unbuttoned his shirt, revealing nothing but a slight gut and hairy chest.

Carter exhaled, relaxing slightly. "I have to take every precaution. I hope you understand," Carter said.

"I do, Carter," Polo responded.

"Now what the fuck would make you turn into a federal snitch, Polo?" Carter asked with contempt.

"The muthafucka Estes is a snake. He played the game dirty, young blood. The nigga left me in the middle of the fucking Atlantic in a boat the size of a bathtub. The fucking US Coast Guard pulled me from the water, and guess what they found taped underneath the fucking boat?" Polo paused and shook his head as he rubbed the top of it, clearly stressed from the recollection of events. "Five fucking kilos of cocaine. The nigga set me up. I was going away, and I don't know about you, but I don't want to spend my golden years behind steel and concrete beating my dick to naked photos. I want shrimp and lobster, naked bitches and good pussy, linen suits and ocean views. So I either had to take those years or turn on the nigga that set me up. Estes robbed me and your father for years, giving us bullshit prices and bad coke. We still built an empire off of that shit, and it burned him up. Wetback, Dominican muthafucka tried to put me under the jail, so I turned on him. I'm the master at the double-cross," Polo said.

Carter rubbed his goatee and shook his head. "Damn." Carter didn't condone Polo's method of revenge, but it was his choice. They were grown men, and Polo had made his bed.

"Anybody associated with that scumbag is going down," Polo said.

Carter thought of Monroe. "Money is associated with Estes," he revealed.

"What? Monroe is dead," Polo shot back.

"Estes staged Monroe's death to protect him from the Haitians, Polo. He is very much alive, and he's doing business with Estes," Carter said as he stood to his feet. He began to pace the room.

"I had no idea," Polo said regretfully. "I'd never do anything to destroy The Cartel."

"He's not aligned with The Cartel anymore, Polo. I came here to get a connect from you so that I could take back the streets from Monroe. He wanted out. He wanted to do his own thing," Carter explained.

"And now you're at war with your brother over real estate in Miami," Polo summarized. "He is your brother, Carter, your younger brother. You are his keeper. Me and your daddy were like brothers, and I don't give a fuck what beef we had; I would never bring him harm. You take care of your brothers, Carter."

Guilt weighed down Carter's shoulders, because he had just given Zyir the okay to take care of Monroe.

"Money is out of control. He tried to have my young'un Zyir murked. He's murdering our men, burning our trap houses. . . ."

"He's your brother. Money and Zyir aren't fighting over money, drugs, turf. . . . They're fighting over you. They both want to be at your right. You've got to make them realize that they both are equally valuable to you. You're the oldest; you can dead the beef," Polo said, cutting off Carter. "Monroe and your friend Zyir will follow by your example. You have the power to remedy things, but whether you do or not, chances are the war will be over soon. I hate to say this, but Monroe is under scrutiny of the Feds. There is no way that he can make it out of this one, and unless you want to see him spend his life behind bars, you have to warn him."

"You should have warned us all, Polo," Carter answered.

Polo stood to his feet and placed his fedora hat back on his head.

"I'm sorry, Carter. I've still got some connections in South America and a few over in Asia. These are safe; nobody knows about these," he said as he wrote down contact information for Carter. "These connects make Estes's coke look like baby powder."

"Is this a setup?" Carter asked, disappointed that someone so thorough had turned informant.

"No, Carter, this is the real deal, baby boy," Polo replied. He looked at Carter with sympathetic eyes. "Take care of your brother. Get him out of the country as soon as possible. They have been building this case against Estes for four years. Money doesn't want to be anywhere near Estes when the other shoe drops."

Chapter 22

"The massacre reminded her
of her father's funeral."
—Unknown

Leena sat at the vanity mirror and Breeze stood directly behind her, admiring her beauty.

"You are beautiful," Breeze said as she looked at Leena, who was dolled up and looking glamorous. It was the day of Leena and Monroe's wedding. The sun shone beautifully and was the making of a fairytale day for Leena. Breeze stroke her hair and smiled at her, giving her approval.

"Are you ready for this big step?" Breeze asked as genuine joy was in her heart for her brother and his soon-to-be wife.

"Yes. I am," Leena said and smiled at Breeze. Just as the words came out of her mouth, they were interrupted. Little Monroe came running into the room with his tuxedo on, looking more like his father than ever. Breeze grabbed him up playfully and kissed him on the cheek.

"Where you think you going, li'l man?" she asked as she beamed from ear to ear. He playfully laughed, and she put him back down and began to fix his bowtie. "You look so handsome, Mr. Diamond," she added. When she looked at little Monroe, she not only saw the resemblance with big Monroe; she saw all of the three men she lost: her father, Mecca, and Monroe. The realization that her whole family had crumbled hit her. She felt the tears begin to build in her eyes, thinking about what the Diamond family had endured.

The sound of a car horn blew, and all of their attention immediately went to the window and snapped Breeze out of her sad thoughts.

Breeze looked out of the window and saw that the car service had arrived. "Okay, it's time to go," Breeze said as she looked at Leena. Leena took a nervous, deep breath and returned the smile.

"I'm ready," she said. With that, they left to head to the wedding.

A tall, well-built driver with a suit and shades waited by the car, the back door open for them. Breeze held the back of Leena's dress to prevent it from dragging on the ground, and Leena had little Monroe in her arms as they made their way to the car. They got into the SUV and headed to the site of the big wedding.

***

Monroe fixed his bowtie in the mirror as his goons stood around him. His black-on-black tuxedo was tailor fit, and it flawlessly hung on his shoulders. He looked sharp, resembling a black James Bond, but even more debonair.

Monroe looked around, and it hit him like a ton of bricks. He was around a whole bunch of niggas who were not family. He knew they were all there because they were working for him. None of them were there on the strength of love for him. It was his wedding day, and he was surrounded by shooters rather than his brothers.

"You ready, big homie?" one of the Opa-locka goons asked.

"Yeah, just ready to get this over with," he said as he checked his cufflinks. Just as he was doing so, Estes walked in. Monroe looked at his crew and gave them a nod, signaling them to leave the room. Almost instantly they filed out of the room, each of them greeting Estes on their way out, out of respect.

"Grandson, today is your big day," Estes said as he walked up to Monroe and straightened up his shirt and his bowtie perfectly.

"Yeah, I can't lie. I'm kind of nervous," Monroe said, being truthful with his grandfather.

Estes chuckled as he rested his hand on Monroe's shoulder to provide his support. "You know what? Years ago, your father said the same thing on the day that he married my daughter. Don't be nervous, son. You are doing the right thing by your family and stepping up to the plate as a man—an honorable man. I just wish your mother and father were here to see you today. They would have been so proud of you today," Estes lectured as he released a rare smile.

"I know that they would have," Monroe said as he returned the smile. "I love you, Grandfather," Monroe said. The two men embraced, and Monroe heard the music begin playing to serenade the few guests who attended the wedding. "I guess that's my cue," Monroe said as he looked back toward the door.

"Let's go," Estes said as he put his arm around Monroe.

They both headed to the front of the ceremony where the priest was waiting. Abruptly, Estes went to the back, having to take a leak before the ceremony started.

✳✳✳

"Wait. Isn't the wedding that way?" Leena asked as she pointed at the southbound interstate sign.

"Yeah, you right," Breeze said as she looked out the window, noticing that they were going the wrong way. "Excuse me, sir. You are going the wrong way. We need to be going south," Breeze said as she yelled to the front.

It seemed as if the driver didn't hear her, because he didn't flinch or respond. He just acted as if she wasn't there.

"Excuse me!" Breeze said, and rang her voice a level higher. The response was just the same . . . nothing. At this point, they knew something was wrong.

"Pull this car over right now!' Breeze yelled as she looked on in disbelief.

The driver finally acknowledged Breeze and looked at her through the rearview mirror. "Look, ma'am, I can't do that," he said with a respectful tone.

"What the hell you mean, you can't?" Leena chimed in as she was trying to figure out what was going on.

"The man who hired me gave me specific instructions. He said drive as far from the wedding as possible. Take it up with him," the driver said, trying to get the women off of his back.

Zyir made the driving arrangements. He had a plan, and to execute it he needed Breeze out of harm's way.

"What? My wedding starts in thirty minutes! You need to turn your ass around and get me there!" Leena yelled as she began to burn from the inside out.

The driver was following orders, but with the two women in his ear nagging him, he knew that it was smart to take them where they requested. He turned around and headed to the wedding site. Little did they know, they were walking straight into a bullet-filled melee.

***

The wedding setup was beautiful and elegant. It was outside, and everything was draped in white. A live band serenaded the guests, and slow jazz filled the air as a crooner began to zat flawlessly.

Zyir's goons were scattered throughout the crowd, including Fly Boogie, who was trying to stay low key in the back row. He had a Tech tucked inside of his tuxedo jacket. His black shades did little to hide his identity, but at that point he didn't care. He was just ready to get the party started. On top of the people in the audience, Zyir had shooters pretending to be waiters.

Little did Monroe know, he had walked into a big booby trap. Monroe walked up to the front of the crowd and stood next to the preacher, who held a Bible in his left hand. The wedding was scheduled to start in five minutes. Everyone was just waiting on the bride to show up . . . but Zyir had a different plan for that particular day.

Zyir also sat in the back, hoping not to get noticed before he gave the signal for hell to break loose. He wanted Monroe and his crew dead. Zyir had just put a major chess move on Monroe, and with Carter's blessing it was about to go down.

Zyir looked across the room and nodded at Fly Boogie. That was all Fly Boogie needed to let the pandemonium begin. He stood up and whipped out the Tech that he had concealed. He instantly pointed to the whole front row and let it off, hitting four of Monroe's goons with one sweep, Fly Boogie was getting busy.

Just as planned, Zyir's other shooters pulled out their guns and began hitting anybody who didn't come in with them. The sounds of thundering blast and bullets whizzing filled the air, and the place went into a complete frenzy.

Monroe ducked down and immediately looked for Estes. However, it was pointless, because Zyir had locked him in the restroom, not wanting to bring any more pain to Breeze's heart. He opted not to kill the grandfather, but everyone else was fair game. He came there on that day for blood, and he was not taking any shorts.

Zyir immediately began to let off shots at Monroe, trying to take his head off. Monroe, never slipping, reached and grabbed the small-caliber gun from the inside pocket of his tux and began to bust back as he took cover.

The massacre had begun as the bodies began to drop and bleed. Zyir's crew and Monroe's were trading bullets, and it was a complete war zone.

Throughout all of the chaos, Monroe and Zyir were busting shots at each other, trying to kill one another. In the meantime, bodies were dropping like flies. The pastor even caught a stray bullet to the abdomen as the two sides went all out against each other.

The shootout went on for seven minutes straight as the killers tried to kill the killers. The gunfire gradually thinned out, and only two guns were being shot—Monroe's and Zyir's. They traded bullets with each other, neither of them hitting anything. Zyir used the corner of the outhouse as a shield, while Monroe ducked behind the stage and used that as his fort. They were trying to take each other's heads off.

Zyir looked around and saw all of the dead bodies. Some of his soldiers were dead, and some of Monroe's were too. He saw Fly Boogie hiding behind a tree with his gun close to his chest. Zyir looked over and they made eye contact. Fly Boogie signaled that he had no more bullets, and Zyir nodded his head and signaled for him to stay put.

Zyir looked at his gun, which was jammed back, and realized that he had run out of bullets. He was a sitting duck at that point, and it would be damn near impossible for him to escape without someone covering him. Zyir, out of pure adrenaline, stepped out in the open with his arms out.

"Monroe!" he yelled. "Bring yo' bitch ass out right now!" Zyir was now in the middle of the floor, stepping in between all of the dead bodies. Just as he figured, Monroe popped up with his gun drawn. He knew that Monroe's ego wouldn't let him stay hidden behind the stage.

Zyir racked his gun back and made it seem as if he had more ammunition, but he was taking his chances bluffing. Monroe and Zyir slowly walked toward each other, meeting in the middle of the floor. They both had their guns pointed at each other, both of them out of bullets while trying to bluff the other. As they both looked down the barrel of a gun, so much hatred was in their hearts as they stared intensely at the man who stood before them.

"You come in here on my wedding day trying to kill me?" Monroe asked through his clenched teeth. He was burning with anger toward Zyir for having the audacity.

"Yeah, and I'm not done yet," Zyir said smoothly as he gripped his gun tightly and returned the screw-face toward Monroe.

Just as Monroe was about to respond, they had guests walk through the door. Leena, his son, and Breeze walked in and witnessed the bloodbath that was supposed to be a joyful day.

"Oh my God," Leena said as she placed her hand over her mouth. Leena quickly grabbed little Monroe and rushed him back out, not wanting him to see the gory sight.

Breeze was frozen in terror as she stopped in her tracks. It reminded her of her father's funeral. It was a complete massacre. Breeze then focused her attention on the two men at the center of the floor, both with guns drawn on each other.

"Zyir! Monroe! No! Stop right now!" Breeze yelled as she stormed toward the two. "Put the guns down now. Please, I'm begging the two of you! Look at all of this. Look what you two have done," she said as her voice began to crack. She was pleading with all of her heart.

Monroe was the first to look away, and when he saw Breeze crying, it hurt him deeply. She fell to her knees and folded her hands in a praying position.

"Please stop, you two. Please! I have lost everything and everyone. I can't take it anymore. I can't!" she said as the tears began to flow down freely and in abundance.

Zyir briefly took his eyes off of Monroe and looked at his wife crying. It broke his heart to see his wife in so much agony. His heart softened temporarily, and he looked back at Monroe, who was in the same spot.

"I'll see you again," Zyir whispered in a low tone that only Monroe would be able to hear.

"Indeed, bitch-ass nigga," Monroe responded with a smile.

With that, Monroe fled the scene. Zyir watched him leave and then lowered his gun. He immediately went over to Breeze, who was completely broken down, sobbing. Zyir walked over to her and tried to console her. He helped her to her feet, and she immediately hauled off and slapped him.

"How could you!" she yelled. Zyir stumbled to the ground and fell on one knee. Breeze knew that she wasn't that powerful, so she looked closer and saw a bloodstain forming in Zyir's abdominal area. He had

caught a bullet from the crossfire, and due to adrenaline, never noticed it. "Zyir!' she yelled as he grimaced
and held his stomach in pain.

✳✳✳

Miamor sat across the table from Murder, frustrated
with her plastic fork and butter knife. She tried to cut
the steak that Murder had prepared for her, but the
utensils broke for the second time. "Can you at least cut
the fucking steak up for me since I can't have a knife?"
she asked as she looked at Murder with hateful eyes
and resentment. Murder shook his head in disbelief
and reluctantly got up and walked over to Miamor. He
cut her steak into pieces for her and quickly returned
to his seat.

"There you go, eat up," he encouraged as he slid a
piece of steak into his mouth.

"You could have given me the knife. I can cut my own
steak," Miamor said as she shook her head and took a
bite of her food.

Murder chuckled and shook his head. "Really? You
think I would give you a knife right now? If it were
any other chick . . . maybe. But you can make a knife
a deadly weapon. I'm not letting that growing belly
over there fool me. You're not some weak pregnant
chick, li'l mama. I know how you get down, Miamor.
Remember, I taught you," Murder said, killing any
thought of Miamor doing any slick stuff that she was
conjuring up in her mind.

Abruptly, Miamor doubled over in pain, grabbing
her stomach. Murder smiled and ignored her, knowing
that she was trying to be deceiving. But when she yelled
out in pain and knocked her plate to the floor, causing
it to shatter, he grew concerned.

Miamor fell to her knees while cupping her baby in agony. Murder looked at her face and saw that she began to sweat profusely, and at that point, he knew that she wasn't faking but being sincere. Murder instantly got up and went over to Miamor's aid. Although he was holding her against her will, he wanted nothing but the best for her. He couldn't stand to see her hurt.

She was on her hands and knees, grimacing in pain as she breathed heavily. Murder then dropped to his knees and removed her hair from in front of her face.

"What's wrong? Are you okay?" he asked as a look of concern was plastered all over his face.

Miamor was sweating and drool was sliding out of her mouth as she attempted to look in Murder's eyes.

"Are you okay?" he asked again as he put his hand on her back. He never saw it coming. Miamor had grabbed a sharp piece of the shattered plate, and with all her might, she jammed the sharp end into Murder's neck.

She let off a roar as she plunged it as deep and hard as she could. Murder instantly grabbed his neck with both hands, and blood began to leak from his mouth. He gagged, not being able to breathe, as his eyes got as big as two golf balls.

Miamor scurried away from him as he reached for her, almost as if he was saying, "help me." She stood to her feet and quickly grabbed the keys that were on his belt buckle. Murder was dying slowly, and Miamor had tears well up in her eyes as she snatched the keys from him and ran to the door.

Murder repeatedly gasped for breath as he slowly crawled over to Miamor as she tried to figure out which key went to each lock. The piece of glass lodged in his throat blocked his airway, and he began to slip in and out of consciousness.

Miamor finally got the locks unlocked and exited the house and ran for dear life, all while Murder was choking on his own blood. Just before he reached his last breath, he mumbled four words. It was four words that he meant with all of his heart. "I love you, Miamor."

Chapter 23

*"If the shoe was on the other foot,
I'd be in the basement morgue."*
                                    —Zyir

Things seemed to move in slow motion as Breeze sat with her face in her palms, bent over in worry as blue scrubs rushed in numerous directions around her. She hated everything about the hospital. Its sterile scent made her stomach turn, the pale white walls were numbingly disgusting. She had seen one too many hospitals, laid in one too many electric beds, met one too many nurses. If she never stepped foot inside another hospital again she could die a happy woman.

She had been sitting for hours, waiting impatiently as her foot did a tap dance against the tiled floor. A mixture of anger and concern brewed inside of her chest. There had been so much blood. Zyir had been in so much pain. *God, please be with him. If something happens to him, I'll die. . . .*

"Are you the young woman that came in with Zyir Rich?"

Her prayers were interrupted by a young black girl with a fresh doobie wrap and a friendly smile. Breeze looked up.

"Yes, I'm his wife . . . Breeze," she said quickly, eagerly. Her desperation was apparent. "Is he okay? Is he out of surgery? Please tell me something. I've been sitting here for hours. No one will tell me anything."

"I'm Nurse Jackie," the girl responded. "Zyir is out of surgery, and the doctors did a wonderful job. They removed the bullet and repaired most of the damage. He will need to stay here for about a week, but he is very lucky."

Breeze placed a hand over her chest and breathed a sigh of relief.

"Can I see him?" she asked.

Before she received an answer, sirens rang out and a group of nurses and doctors rushed to the ER doors.

"Jackie, get over here. We've got one coming in!" one of the doctors yelled to the young girl standing before Breeze.

"I'm sorry. I've got to go. Someone will come for you when you can see him," the girl yelled as she ran across the room.

Breeze walked toward the commotion as she watched the girl jump into the action. The doctors and nurses transferred a body from the back of an ambulance onto a gurney and wheeled it quickly past Breeze.

"This woman is in pre-term labor and the baby's heartbeat is weakening. We've got to get this baby out of her now!" a doctor yelled.

Breeze looked at the face on the gurney and her mouth fell open in shock. She chased after the group of doctors and nurses. "Wait!" she yelled.

"Please, ma'am, someone will be out to inform you about your husband," Nurse Jackie said urgently.

"But wait! I know her! She's my—"

Before Breeze could finish her sentence, they had wheeled their patient into a restricted area, leaving Breeze standing in the hallway distraught. She stormed out of the hospital and into the parking lot, where she pulled out her phone.

"Please answer, please answer," she mumbled as she dialed Carter's number.

"Hello?"

As soon as she heard his voice, she began to cry. "Carter! You have to come home. Everything is out of control. Money shot Zyir. There was a big shootout. We need you here. I found . . ." She swallowed the lump in her throat. "I found Miamor."

✳✳✳

Carter boarded his jet with urgency as he nodded a greeting to the pilot. "Let's get her in the air as soon as possible. I need to get back to Miami immediately," Carter instructed.

"I think they might slow things down," the pilot responded. Carter turned to him in confusion, and the pilot pointed to the red and blue lights that were racing toward Carter's jet. The unmarked black vehicles were filled with federal agents, and Carter's worst fear had come to fruition.

Visiting Polo had been a mistake. There was no doubt in his mind that Polo had kept his promise by not speaking about The Cartel to the Feds, but just by showing up at his door, he knew that he was now on the radar of the government. Carter had been down this road before. He wasn't trying to catch another case, especially a fed case.

"Start the engine," Carter said as he stepped off of the plane.

One agent approached him, yelling over the whir of the plane's propellers. "Carter Jones!" he shouted as he flashed his badge. "Agent Cooper. I can't let you get on this plane."

"Considering that your cuffs aren't out and your men don't have their guns drawn I'd say that you don't have a warrant," Carter said calmly as he tucked his hands in his designer slacks and stood shoulders squared in front of the agent. "Now I'm going to get on this plane and fly back to Miami, and you will forget that you ever saw my face, if you know what's good for you. Do your homework, Agent Cooper. You can't beat me." Carter patted the agent on the shoulder as if to say, "Better luck next time." He then turned and ascended the steps to his jet without ever letting the pig mu'fuckas below him see him sweat.

✳✳✳

Carter could face a thousand-man army, stare down the Feds, or take on any other kingpin without batting an eye, but when it came to seeing Miamor, he couldn't handle it. He walked into the dark hospital room and saw her resting peacefully. He didn't understand exactly what had occurred, but he was grateful to see her nonetheless.

He looked at her flattened abdomen and knew that she had told the truth in her letter. She had aborted the baby, his baby, and he had to bite his inner jaw to contain his sadness. Why couldn't she just be the woman he expected her to be? What was it that made her so cold, so disloyal when it came to him? And despite all of this, why couldn't he ever let her go? He couldn't get her out of his system. Whenever she beckoned, he came running to her rescue, no matter what kind of hurt she had put on his heart. Carter couldn't figure out why his heart wanted her so badly.

Nurse Jackie walked into the room.

"She's strong," Nurse Jackie said.

Carter nodded his head. "She is," he agreed with a sarcastic scoff.

"You must be the child's father? He's in the nursery. He's small and very fragile, but he's strong, too. Not many babies survive being born three months early, but he's a fighter. Would you like to see him?" the nurse asked.

Carter looked at her as if she were speaking French. He looked back at Miamor and then to the nurse. "She had the baby?"

"Yes, she had him a few hours ago. That's why she's so exhausted. She's probably on Mars right now because of all the pain medication she's on, but she'll wake up when she's good and rested. She did good today. She almost lost your son, and she cussed the doctors out every step of the way, until she heard his screams," Nurse Jackie said.

Carter leaned over and kissed Miamor's forehead then whispered in her ear, "Thank you."

"Come on, I'll take you to see him," the nurse offered.

Carter followed the nurse to the neonatal intensive care unit where the premature babies were taken care of, and as soon as he rounded the corner he saw Breeze. She sat in a rocking chair, holding his son, singing softly in his ear.

Carter could barely keep his composure. He fought tears of joy as he approached his sister. Breeze looked up and smiled. She put a finger up over her lips to request silence.

"Congratulations, Carter, I'd like you to meet your baby boy," Breeze said as she handed the tiny bundle of joy to his father.

The connection that Carter felt when he held his son caused his heart to swell. "He's so small," Carter said.

"He'll grow big and strong. We'll have to keep him here for a while—"

"No, he's coming home. I'll hire the best doctors and nursing staff to be with him around the clock if I have to, but when his mother leaves the hospital, so will he," Carter said with authority. He looked down at his trooper with all the love and happiness in the world. He had never felt so complete. The little dude was a true blend of his parents; he was the perfection that resulted from all of their imperfection. Out of all the bad that they had done in their lives, he was the one right that fixed them all.

"Daddy loves you, man," Carter said with sincerity.

The nurse took him and placed him back in the incubator, handling him with the gentlest of care.

"This will keep him away from things that can harm him. He's very delicate, and his lungs still have to mature. We'll keep him hooked up to machines that will help him breathe and monitor his heart rhythms until we're sure that he can function without them," the nurse explained.

"Can we have him moved to Miamor's room? I want them together at all times," Carter explained. He looked to Breeze. "And call up Fly Boogie. I need a man on her door around the clock until I can get her home. How is Zyir?" Carter asked.

"I haven't been in to see him yet," Breeze said.

"What?" Carter exclaimed, surprised.

"He and Money would have killed each other if Leena and I hadn't shown up. You should have seen them, Carter. I can't even look at Zyir right now or Monroe," Breeze said as she shook her head in disgrace.

"I'll go in and have a talk with him first, but he needs you right now, B. So get yourself together. The last thing he needs is his wife against him too," Carter said. He kissed her cheek and then held her hand as they walked toward Zyir's room.

Carter entered the hospital room and saw Zyir lying with his head against a pillow, eyes open, face solemn.

"What's good, Zy? How you hanging in there?" Carter asked.

"Shit hurts like a mu'fucka, fam," Zyir stated. "They talking about keeping me for a week."

"You need anything? You comfortable in here? I can send you home, set you up with a nurse and everything if you want. Just say the word, li'l homie," Carter offered.

"Nah, the way B is acting, home might be a little chilly, nah mean?" Zyir replied.

Breeze opened the door and stepped inside, keeping her distance as she looked at Zyir.

"You alive?" Breeze asked.

"Yeah, B, I'm breathing," Zyir answered with a charming smile and a wink.

Breeze shifted uncomfortably in her stance. "If I hadn't stopped you, would you have killed him?" she asked.

Zyir knew that his answer could change the course of their relationship, but he didn't want to lie to Breeze. He owed her more than that. He had spoken nothing but truth to her since they first met. He wouldn't start lying now. "If I had the best draw, yes. If the shoe was on the other foot, I'd be in the basement morgue," he said.

"I won't stay around and watch you put my brother in a casket, Zyir. I will not bury another person with the last name Diamond, and if you make me, I will hate you until the day I take my last breath. You end the beef with Money and I'll come home," she said as she slipped her five-carat wedding ring off her finger. "Until then you can have this back." She set the ring on the foot of the bed and rushed out of the room before he could see her tears.

Zyir grimaced as he reached down and picked up the ring. He held it inside his hand as he brought his closed fist to his mouth and kissed it. He looked at Carter, who gave him a gentle pat on the back.

"Looks like I don't got a choice, fam. I better get comfortable in this hospital bed, because I may not have a home to go back to."

✳✳✳

"Get off of me!" Leena screamed as she snatched her arm away from Monroe as he ushered her into the house.

"I want niggas all around the house," he shouted to his three most trusted henchmen as he breathed hard and his eyes lit up in anger. "Niggas on the roof and around the perimeter. If Carter or Zyir even drive past this house, blow them straight to fucking hell!" he barked.

Leena covered her son's ears as she rocked him in her arms. "Money, just stop it! Do you hear yourself? You sound insane! Have you lost your fucking mind?" she asked. Her once beautiful white dress was covered in blood. What was supposed to be the happiest day of her life had turned into the worst. "This was our wedding day!"

"The nigga Zyir is out of his league. He ruined your day, not me! He started it, but I'ma finish it and snatch the fucking crown off of his dead head. I'm going to hang the disrespectful nigga from the fucking street-lights," Monroe barked.

Leena stormed out of the room enraged as she carried her son to his room. She marched into the master bedroom and pulled out a suitcase, stuffing clothes, jewelry, and shoes inside sloppily as tears flowed down her cheeks. She was fed up. The people she loved were fighting like enemies on the street.

She grabbed the Louis Vuitton luggage and wheeled it back to the living room. Monroe turned toward her, confused.

"I know you're mad, Lee, but where you going? Huh? You're not going anywhere, baby," he said, softening his tone.

Leena smirked and snaked her neck like only a black girl can do. "You fucking right I'm not going anywhere. You are. Take your shit, Money, and leave. You want to beef with Zyir. You two want to kill each other, you can do it without me. I won't watch that. I won't stick around for the bullshit," she said.

"Lee, there are some things you don't understand."

"Just leave, Money," she said with hurt eyes and with defeat lacing her tone.

"Leena," Monroe said more sternly this time.

"Get out! And take your goons with you!"

Monroe stormed out of the house, and it took everything in Leena not to call him back. He didn't even turn around before slamming the door to their home, and as soon as he disappeared from her sight, Leena dropped to the floor in devastation. She cried her woes of despair, drowning in a heap of lace and sadness as she prayed for a resolution to a winless war.

✳✳✳

When Miamor opened her eyes, Carter's was the first face that she saw.

"Hey, you," she said with a lazy smile as tears came to her eyes. "I didn't think I'd ever see you again."

Carter leaned down and kissed her dry lips. "Why did you run from me?" he asked.

Miamor frowned and shook her head in protest. "I would never run from you, Carter. A nigga snatched me off the street in broad daylight. My old boyfriend.

Someone I knew from my past took me," she whispered.

"Did he touch you?" Carter asked. "What old boyfriend, ma? What's the nigga name?" Carter spit venom with each word he spoke as Miamor saw flames of anger dancing in his eyes.

"He didn't touch me, but I don't think he had any intention of ever letting me go," she answered honestly. "We used to be close. He went to jail years ago and I forgot about him. I met you, and I left him in my past. I guess he didn't want to stay there."

"What's his name?" Carter asked again.

"Murder," she replied.

"What about the letter?" he asked. "He made you write that too?"

"I don't know anything about a letter," Miamor replied. "The first opportunity I got, I ran. I stabbed him and I took off. I didn't look back. I don't know if he's dead or alive. I just kept running until I couldn't anymore. He's the only person besides Mecca that I've ever been afraid of. What if he's not dead?"

Carter was livid as he saw the fear and heard the anxiety in her voice. "Don't worry yourself, ma. I'll handle it. He won't ever touch you again. Just lay back and rest. You've done enough work. You did good, kid. You gave me the greatest gift . . . my son. I'll protect you both at all costs. I love you."

He kissed her once more then sat back in deep contemplation as she drifted into a restless sleep.

Chapter 24

"No Guns. No Goons. Just me and you."
                                        —Carter

Carter looked in his rearview mirror and noticed that the same two cars had been following him for blocks. At that moment, he knew that the Feds were on him. The white boys who were driving the cars that were tailing him were a dead giveaway. Carter immediately put the pedal to the metal and bent a couple corners to shake them. With his foreign car and world-class speed, there was no competition.

Carter checked his rearview mirrors after a couple corners and brief stretches and just as he expected, he was in the clear. He headed toward the hospital for Zyir. It was a must that they shook out of town until things died down. The heat from the authorities was too much to bear.

As Carter made his way toward the hospital, his phone began to ring. He looked down at his caller ID and noticed that the call originated from Los Angeles, California. He picked it up, only to hear another person breathing on the phone.

"Hello," he said again and still received no answer. He then knew that the call was coming from Polo. It was a discreet way of telling Carter that the Feds were about to move in on him.

Carter hung up his phone and shook his head in frustration. He knew that if he stayed around, it was only a matter of time before he went down. First and foremost, he had to get his li'l man out of the city too. Zyir was his right-hand man from day one, and he refused to flee the city and leave Zyir hanging out to dry.

Carter arrived at the hospital and immediately knew that he would be walking into a trap. He could spot unmarked cars from a mile away, and the entrances were swarmed with them.

"Fuck!" he said as he hit his steering wheel with force and aggression. He picked up his phone and called Zyir.

"Hello," Zyir answered in a low, raspy tone.

"Listen, who is in there with you?" Carter asked, cutting straight to the point.

"Just me and Fly Boogie," Zyir said as he slowly sat up in the bed while grimacing.

"Listen closely, because we don't have a lot of time. The Feds are coming in. Do me a favor. Tell Boogie to look outside the door and see if there are any agents outside your door," Carter said as he pulled off and looked at the cop cars filing into the hospital through his rearview mirror.

Zyir immediately told Fly Boogie to check, and he poked his head outside of the door and came back.

"It looks clear. Just a couple of nurses," he said as he stood there wide-eyed, trying to figure out what was about to go down.

"Shit looks normal," Zyir said to Carter.

"Okay, good, good. That means that they are on their way to you right now. Listen, you have to get the fuck out of there, Zyir. Like right now," Carter said.

"Damn. Okay, cool. Where are you at?" Zyir answered.

"Meet me at the take-off spot. You already know what it is," Carter said, not wanting to tip off anyone, just in case he had wiretaps on his phone.

"On my way," Zyir said as he began to snatch the wires off of him that were monitoring his heart rate.

"Yo, Zyir," Carter said as his tone dropped.

"What up, big homie?" Zyir replied.

"I'm not leaving without you, so make sure you get there," Carter said with all sincerity in his voice.

"I'll be there," Zyir confirmed just before he hung up the phone.

Carter headed in the direction of Monroe's condominium. He had unfinished business with his brother that needed to be handled.

Carter made sure that there wasn't anyone trailing him before he turned into Monroe's place. Carter took his gun from his waist and exited the car. He threw the gun in the seat, not wanting to even have it on him when approaching Monroe. He didn't want to go that route with Monroe. Carter just had to tie up loose ends.

Carter walked to the doorstep and knocked. He didn't know what to expect on the opposite end, but he was prepared for whatever God had in store for him.

As Carter waited for someone to answer, he got a bad feeling in the pit of his stomach. He took a deep breath and then exhaled, trying to calm his nerves.

The sounds of locks being unclicked sounded, and Carter stood strong as he waited for the face of his brother to appear. Once the door was open, he realized that it wasn't a face that he was staring at, but it was the barrel of a double pump shotgun that Monroe was holding about five inches from his nose.

"I come in peace," Carter said as he put both his hands up. Carter walked toward the gun, pressing his chest against the barrel and slowly walking Monroe backward. "I don't want no smoke, bro. Just want to talk," Carter pleaded as he spoke softly, slowly, and collected. There was no hostility showing in his voice or mannerisms. He knew that he was playing Russian roulette at that point, but he knew it had to be resolved.

"You come to my house after you sent ya li'l mans to get me? You must be out of your mind," Monroe said as he stopped and dug the barrel into Carter's chest even deeper.

"You're right. But if I recall right, you sent Buttons' niggas to kill me in Rio. Remember that? Look, we both have been at each other, but this shit has to stop," Carter said with no malice in his heart.

Monroe was at a loss for words.

"I'm tired of the killings. I just want this shit to end. Honestly, I would prefer if you get this gun out of my chest. If you want, I'll shoot you a fair one and we can handle it like men," Carter said, referring to a one-on-one fight. "No guns, no goons. Just me and you," Carter suggested.

Monroe paused as if he was in deep contemplation and then released a small smile, gladly wanting to take Carter up on his offer. Monroe slowly lowered the gun and then tossed it on his couch. Carter stepped completely in the house and closed the door behind him. He then took off his shirt, exposing his chiseled body and ripped abs.

"I thought you would never ask, playboy," Monroe said as he snatched off his shirt and put up his hands. They were both the direct bloodline of the most fearless man who ever walked the earth: Carter Diamond. So there was no fear in either one of their hearts.

Carter also put his hands up, and the men began to circle each other in the middle of Monroe's living room.

"This ass whooping has been a long time coming," Carter said as he began to inch closer to his brother.

Monroe threw the first punch. Carter side-stepped to the left, just barely missing getting hit by Monroe's punch. Almost simultaneously, Carter snapped a quick jab to Monroe's kidney.

"Too slow, li'l nigga," Carter said as he smiled and swiped his nose, taunting him. This enraged Monroe.

Monroe began to throw haymakers at Carter, trying to knock his head off. Carter caught a couple of them, but the majority of them he dodged artistically.

Carter saw that Monroe was getting tired, and he knew it was time for him to put in work. He went after Monroe relentlessly. Left hook, right hook, jab—sending Monroe flying onto his back. Carter then pounced on Monroe, straddling him while wrapping both hands around his neck, trying to choke the life out of him.

Monroe fought for air as Carter gripped his neck tightly. Monroe felt that Carter was much stronger than him and knew that he needed help getting Carter off of him. He reached for the lamp and grabbed it. He then smashed it against Carter's head, making the lamp shatter into pieces and temporarily getting Carter off of him.

Carter flew to the ground as the world began to spin. He temporarily saw stars and tried to get up, but couldn't keep his balance.

Monroe, on the other hand, was panting on the ground, trying to catch his breath. Blood leaked from Monroe's swollen lip, and Carter had a huge gash on the right side of his head. It was an awkward moment of silence as both of them leaned their backs against the wall and tried to regain their composure.

"We could have been a dynasty. We . . . could . . ." Monroe tried to say in between breaths as he steadily held his throbbing neck.

"That was the plan," Carter said as he sweated profusely and sucked air, trying to get his wind.

"You let that nigga Zyir take my place," Monroe admitted as he expressed his true feelings. He was envious of the place that Zyir held in his brother's life. They
were close, and Monroe felt as if he had missed out by
being away from life for so long.

"Zyir is my nigga. He's been there with me from the
start. He wasn't taking anyone's place, because he always had a place of his own. So that's what this is all
about, huh?"

"I just believe in blood over everything. I was raised
in this drug game, and what I learned is that anybody
will cross you for the right price. But family, family
doesn't have a price. Family is forever. Diamonds are
forever."

"Diamonds are forever. We have to end this,
Money. We have to," Carter said as he looked over at
Monroe. Neither of them wanted the beef to go any
further. It was as if them saying that Diamonds are
forever released the tension out of the room.

"I've lost everybody from this game. This game has
no love for anyone. I don't want to lose the only brother
I have left behind this," Carter admitted.

"I want this shit to be over too, bro. I swear to God
I do. It seems like it's at a point of no return," Monroe
replied.

"It's never too late, my nigga. All we have to do is let
it end here," Carter said as he slowly stood up, sneering
at his aching headache. He reached down his hand to
Monroe and looked at his brother in the eyes.

Monroe paused and took a long, hard thought about
what he was about to do. He took a deep breath and
reached out his hand, letting his older brother help him
up. They embraced and rocked back and forth, both of
their souls being cleansed in the process.

"Now we have to go. The Feds are coming," Carter said as he went to the window and looked down over the street cautiously. "We have to go. They will be here any minute."

"What?" Monroe asked, trying to grasp what was going on.

"They're on to Estes, which means they're on to all of us. Just come on! I don't have time to explain, but I have a jet waiting to take us to Bermuda. All we have to do is make it to the airstrip. We have to go!" Carter said as he fled out of the door.

Monroe followed closely behind, and just like that, they were gone out of the door.

✳✳✳

Zyir looked at the dashboard and saw Fly Boogie pushing over 120 miles per hour. Zyir then looked in his rearview mirror and saw the trail of police cars and flashing lights. They were on a high-speed chase, and Zyir knew that it wasn't looking good. He looked at Fly Boogie and noticed a grin on his face. He was actually enjoying the high-stakes car chase. A helicopter was hovering above them, keeping up with their every move. Zyir shook his head and had no choice but to smile. He gripped his wounded stomach and felt his phone vibrate. It was Carter.

"I'm on my way, but I have a couple friends with me," Zyir said, knowing that it didn't look good for him.

"I'm waiting for you, homie. You have to get here. I am not leaving without you, Zyir. Make a way," Carter said confidently. He heard the sirens in the background and knew that Zyir wasn't looking too good.

Carter hung up the phone and took a deep breath. He and Monroe were sitting on the jet, waiting to go. Carter looked at his watch and took a deep breath.

"He'll be here," he assured Monroe as he looked out of the window. "Come on, Zy," he whispered to himself.

Fly Boogie jumped off the highway, pushing almost 150 miles per hour. He had created about a thirty-second lead on the cops, and he had an idea. He saw a tunnel and knew that that was their only chance. With the helicopter still on their tail, Fly Boogie raced into the tunnel and stopped about halfway through it.

"Look, big homie, you go that way and I'm going to shoot out this way, taking all them Feds away from you."

"Damn, Boogie. I'm not going to let you go out like that. Fuck it. I'm rolling with you. Let's get it," Zyir said bravely as he steadily clutched his stomach and frowned.

"Naw, I got you, big homie. They want you, not me. I have zero strikes and they have nothing on me. This shit going to make me a legend in the hood," Fly Boogie said as he kept a childish grin on his face.

Zyir shook his head and returned the smile. "You a crazy li'l nigga. You know that?" Zyir said as he held out his hand and gave Boogie a pound.

"And you know this!' he said playfully as he dapped up his mentor.

Zyir got out of the car and began to walk the opposite way. Fly Boogie put the pedal to the metal and shot out of the tunnel like a bat out of hell. He shot out of the tunnel and the helicopter got right back on his tail.

The federal agent in the helicopter called in Fly Boogie's location, and a mile down the road the cops were back on him. This time it was double the amount of marked cars chasing him. Fly Boogie was about to go down like a G.

Zyir casually walked into a gas station that was nearby and used the payphone to call a cab. Within thirty minutes he was pulling up at the jet strip where Carter was waiting for him.

Carter helped him into the jet, and Zyir was startled when he reached the door and saw a hand reaching to help him in. It was Monroe.

Zyir got onto the aircraft, and Carter immediately shut the door. "Okay, let's go!" he yelled to the pilot as they took off.

Carter looked at Zyir and then Monroe. He was determined to bring his family back together, and he was not taking no for an answer. Before they would kill each other, Carter would kill them both. He wanted the war to end for good. They had other problems ahead of them—problems that they could have never forseen. The three biggest gangsters in history were on their ass: The F—B—I.

The jet lifted into the air and disappeared into the clouds as three of the realest niggas in Miami flew off into the sunset. Carter directed the pilot to head directly toward the Bermuda triangle—a no-fly zone where many aircrafts have vanished in American history. He instructed Zyir and Monroe to sit back and relax until they reached their destination. He had a plan—a master plan.

Carter sat back in the luxury chair and stared out of the window. Just before they entered the Bermuda triangle, he smiled and whispered, "Diamonds are forever."

Final Chapter

"I'm numb to the death around by now.
It doesn't even matter."
—Breeze

Weeks Later

Leena lay in bed, holding her son to her chest as she cried her eyes out over Monroe. She had lost him once before, and now she was reliving the horror of his death all over again. *How can a plane just fall out of the sky without anyone noticing? God, please keep them. Bless their souls,* she prayed silently.

The minutes on the clock ticked by, torturously slow as she waited for the sun to break through the dark sky. She needed to speak with Breeze and Miamor. They were all that she had left. Leena felt more vulnerable than ever, and they were the only women in the world who could relate to her pain. Widows of The Cartel, they had more in common now than they ever had before. Through circumstance they had been made sisters, and everything that their men had left behind was now in their hands. Power, paper, prestige . . . an entire empire now lay at their feet.

Leena kissed her son's head, grabbed her cell phone off the nightstand, and rose from the bed. Putting on her silk kimono robe, she walked out onto the balcony that overlooked the entire estate. Monroe had her living in the lap of luxury. Their mansion rested on a ten-acre compound on the outskirts of the city limits. He provided her with the best of everything. From labels to diamonds, she was afforded her heart's desires, but the material things seemed so pointless now. None of it mattered. She would burn the multi-million dollar walls she dwelled in to the ground if it meant Money could live again. What she wanted most was time with the man she loved. It seemed as though life always tore them apart, and for a second time she was mourning his loss.

Her mind was so full and her heart so heavy that she could barely breathe. She felt weighted with emotion, and she needed to get some of it off her chest.

Leena dialed Miamor's number. Full of tension, she didn't even realize that she was holding her breath.

"Leena, why are you awake? It's so late," Miamor answered.

Leena exhaled loudly and chuckled slightly. "I could ask you the same thing. Doesn't sound like you're getting much sleep either."

"The baby is restless. To be honest, so am I. I miss him. I can't believe he's gone," Miamor admitted. "He was all I had left. So what the hell do I do now?"

Leena's heart went out to Miamor. To see Carter and her together was to see true love. Leena knew that not even her own relationship with Monroe could rival the one she witnessed whenever she was around them. "Have you spoken to Breeze?" Leena asked.

The sound of sirens broke through the silent night, and Leena looked around in confusion, and then she looked at her security cameras.

"The police are here," Leena announced. Unmarked black cars were pulling onto her property. "They must've found the plane," Leena whispered as she rushed back into the house, tightening the belt on her

kimono as she raced through the massive mansion. "I'll
call you back," Leena said.

"Lee . . . wait . . ." Miamor began to protest, but
Leena ended the call.

Her feet slapped the cold tile floor as she headed toward the front door, frantically, as hope began to rise
in her broken heart. She flung open the door and ran
out into the yard, meeting the officers in front of her
home before they even got out of their vehicles. She
was taken aback when she saw how many had come. By
the time she realized something was wrong it was too
late. Twenty federal agents exited their vehicles swiftly
with automatic weapons aimed toward her face. Red
beams appeared all over her upper torso, and as Leena
looked down she realized that all it took was an itchy
trigger finger to end her life.

"Let me see your hands! On the ground now!"

Leena went deaf as the thunderous hum of a helicopter roared above her head. The windstorm that it created as it circled above her, shining a bright spotlight
on her, caused her hair to blow wildly.

"What? What is going on?" she shouted frantically.

"Hands up! On the ground now!"

Leena was manhandled to the cement as she resisted
their demands. She watched as the Feds swarmed her
home. "Wait! My son is inside! My son is in the house!"
she screamed as she tried to stand.

One of the men put a forceful knee in her back,
causing her to grimace in pain as he cuffed her wrists
tightly. The metal bit into her skin, and her wrist
snapped from the agent's brute force. They held no
sympathy for her as they made their arrest.

"You can't do this! I've done nothing wrong! My
son! If you touch one hair on his head, I will have your
fucking head!" she screamed as she resisted arrest. She

lunged, kicking and screaming as she tried to break free. All she could think of was her son. Leena had no idea why she was even under arrest, but the Feds had come at her so heavy that she could only assume the worst.

Leena's heart broke in half as they forced her into the car. She looked out of the rearview window and saw her son crying hysterically in the arms of one of the men. She broke down instantly. She had no clue of what would become of her and her child.

"Please, just tell me what is going on. What will happen to my son?" she asked as snot and tears wrecked her pretty face. There was no keeping her composure. Leena was distraught. She knew that the tides of life were changing. With the death of the men, the Feds had grown balls of steel. They would have never come at The Cartel with such arrogance and disrespect otherwise.

"Your son will be placed in temporary custody of the state," one of the Feds said as he drove away from her home.

"No, please! You can't," she said with a gasp.

"We can and we will, unless you can tell us something that will make us change our minds and set you free. Your cooperation will make all of this go away. So do yourself a favor and tell us what you know about the murders, the cocaine, the dirty money laundering that The Cartel is involved in. It's in your best interest to start talking."

✳✳✳

"I'm not telling you anything," Breeze stated as she sat with her hands behind her back, handcuffed to the hard chair.

"We have evidence against you and everyone affiliated with The Cartel. We've got you for drug traffick-
ing, running a criminal enterprise, fraud, tax evasion,
the list goes on and on."

Breeze kept her eyes on the wall in front of her,
barely blinking as she blocked out the voice of the
federal agent. The olive-skinned man leaned in menacingly over Breeze, using intimidation tactics to get her
to break.

Zyir had trained her well. Breeze knew better than to
volunteer any information. They couldn't even get her
prints on a coffee cup, she was so seasoned. Growing
up in the folds of the largest organization in the South
had prepared her for this moment.

"We found pieces of an aircraft, scattered throughout the Atlantic Ocean, about 150 miles off the coast of
Bermuda. Too bad the cowards left their ladies to take
the fall for their bad deeds."

Breeze's eyes turned dark at the insult and her heart
wrenched. "You don't have anything on me," Breeze
said.

"We have everything on you. You recognize this
face?" The agent tossed a photo of Estes onto the table
in front of her, and Breeze turned green as her stomach
turned.

"Let's just say family doesn't mean much these
days. He's singing like a canary and has implicated
not only your husband and brothers, but you and over
a hundred other mid- and low-level dealers across
the state," the agent said. He noticed that Breeze's
demeanor had changed.

"Not so cocky now, huh, princess?" he mocked. "We
picked up over thirty people directly affiliated with The
Cartel. You're standing tall, but do you honestly think
all of them will too? Now the way this works is whoever

talks first gets the deal. There is only one way out of this."

✳✳✳

"Magdalena!" Miamor yelled in urgency as she quickly dressed. The Spanish housekeeper appeared in the doorway. "I need you to watch the baby. Do not let anyone into this house under any circumstances. I don't care if God himself knocks on the door. You don't let anyone in. *Comprende?*"

"Sí, sí," Magdalena replied.

Miamor placed a call to Carter's attorney and within minutes she was headed to the federal building. She knew the game, and now that the Feds felt The Cartel was weakened, they were coming in for the kill. There was no way that Miamor was letting all that Carter had built be destroyed. She had watched him closely, studied the way that he reigned, and just as she had in life, she would now hold him down in death. She already knew that Leena had been arrested, and when she couldn't reach Breeze, she had a gut feeling that she was being held too. Surely they had intended to come for her next, but Miamor moved to her own beat. She wasn't being taken into custody without representation.

She rode in the back of the plush interior of the Maybach as her driver guided it through the city's streets. Miamor's chest heaved as anxiety crept into her bones. Today her worst fear was coming true. She was about to go up against the law. Most who did it had no wins, but with the team of sharks that Carter had left her with she was confident that she could come out of things unscathed.

The car arrived at her destination and Miamor saw that Carter's legal team was waiting at the top of the steps. Steve Rosenberg, the best esquire in the city, was already on retainer. Standing confident and dapper as ever in a Brooks Brothers suit, he waited with a briefcase in hand. Miamor waited for her driver to open her door, then she emerged from the vehicle.

"Ms. Matthews, I'm glad you were smart enough to call me," he said as she shook his hand.

"Thank you for coming, Mr. Rosenberg," she replied anxiously.

"Looks like they're reaching a bit. They do have extensive evidence on Carter, Zyir, and Monroe, but seeing as though they are now deceased, that pigeonholes their investigation. They're using scare tactics to try and get an informant out of you ladies. The Cartel has been responsible for drugs and crime in this city. They need a kingpin to tie it to, but in this case they are willing to settle for a queen pin. Since they can't get your men, they now are gunning for the three of you."

"They have Leena and Breeze. Have they turned them?" Miamor asked as she bit her inner jaw, hoping that the ladies could stand tall under pressure.

"Not yet, but let's go get them out of there before one of them do. The DEA has been known to flip the most hardened of criminals."

Just seeing the face of such a prestigious defense attorney turned to tables in the girls' favor. Within an hour Breeze and Leena were released, but the struggle was far from over.

"They'll keep coming for you. As long as they have Estes's cooperation, it's only a matter of time before they bring indictments down on anyone he's naming. I'll do more research in the morning to find out what we're up against. I'll be in touch," Rosenberg said.

"What about my son?" Leena asked urgently.

"I've already made arrangements to have him returned to you. As soon as they process the paperwork, a caseworker will drop him off to your home. Shouldn't take more than a few hours."

He bid adieu to the ladies, and they each watched him pull away.

"They found the plane," Breeze informed sadly as tears flooded her eyes. "It crashed in the middle of the ocean. Divers are still looking for their bodies."

"What are we going to do? Everything is falling apart," Leena whispered.

The three women formed a small circle and put their arms around one another, creating a circle of power . . . street royalty. They were the queens who would inherit the throne.

"We do what we have to do. We take over The Cartel," Miamor replied. "And the first thing on the agenda is to clear our names." She turned sympathetically toward Breeze. "I know that Estes is your grandfather, but—"

Breeze put her hand up and interrupted. "Do what needs to be done. If he's talking, it'll be well deserved anyway. I'm numb to the death around by now. It doesn't even matter."

"Do you guys know what this means? We can't just step in their shoes. I just sat back and spent the money. I'm not in the streets. I don't know the first thing about running anything . . . I can't do this," Leena protested.

"You can and you will. For years we've sat back and watched the throne. It's time we inherited it. It is our time now, ladies, and we either do this together or watch the entire Cartel fall. The vultures will pick everything our men established apart until there's nothing left if we don't assume our roles," Miamor schooled. She knew the streets. She had come up in the trenches, and her murder game was official. There was nothing in her that was scared of this opportunity. She was reveling at the chance to continue Carter's legacy.

"We have no muscle," Breeze said.

"Some will stay loyal; others will test us. Niggas gonna learn a hard lesson when they buck, but they not knocking us off," Miamor assured.

"First we memorialize our men. Give them a homegoing that the streets will never forget," Leena whispered.

Breeze nodded and added, "Then the takeover begins."

TO BE CONTINUED . . .

The Cartel V: *La Bella Mafia*

Coming up next from our camp . . .
The Day the Streets Stood Still by JaQuavis Coleman (December 24, 2012)
The Prada Plan 3 by Ashley Antoinette (January 29, 2013)
Pre-order today! Visit www.ashleyjaquavis.com

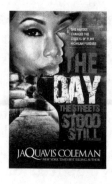